ECHOES
IN THE STORM

Cover Image: Wander Aguiar
Cover Model: Andrew Biernat
Cover design: Max Effect
Editing: Lauren Clarke
Formatting: Max Effect

For those whose past mistakes
weigh heavy on their heart.

Your failures do not define you,
nor should your regrets.

For without these,
how are we to grow?

ONE

CAMMIE

Eleven hours in the office, and this is what I have to come home to. I close my eyes and focus on my breathing, trapped in the naïve thought that maybe, just maybe, if I wish him away hard enough, it could truly happen.

Nope. Still there.

My ex leans a shoulder against the house, tucked under the veranda as though he had hoped to blend into the shadows and catch me by surprise.

Blondie belts a tune out on my car radio, the beat going some way toward helping me find my Zen. Three years on, and the sheer sight of him still pisses me off, the same as it did when he told me "I don't think I can ever love you again."

Yeah. Because loving me means accepting the fact it wasn't my fault, and he refuses to believe that.

I refuse to believe that.

Drawing a deep breath, I reach for the door handle and promptly cut Blondie off mid-sentence as the crisp evening air rushes in to my safe haven. With my leather tote snatched in my other hand, I rise and plaster on as natural a smile as I can manage when my back aches and my feet throb from overuse.

"Eight months, Jared."

"And yet, it hasn't dulled your attitude any." He looks down his nose at me as I approach, arms folded across his chest.

"What do you want?" I lock the car, pining for that first dip of my feet into a hot bath.

"You ignored my calls." He frowns as I walk right by him. "Did you think I'd be that easy to brush off?"

"Hardly." There was a reason he used to be saved in my phone under 'Cockroach'. "I've been busy."

"You're not the only one," he bites, inviting himself into the house behind me. "But then again, you never did understand that concept, did you?"

"Carry on, Jared," I snap louder than intended. "See how long this wee conversation lasts if that's the way you're going to steer it."

He pinches the bridge of his nose and sighs. "I'll make it quick." For a fleeting second, I see the vulnerable man I fell in love with ten years ago. "I want you to sell the house."

Until that.

"What?" I throw my tote on the side table with more zest than necessary.

We were married for barely two years, not enough time for the property to have increased substantially in value. So it was decided when we split that I'd stay in it, paying the mortgage on my own, and the little that he had put in over the course of our relationship would be repaid when I sold.

When I sold.

"If you need the cash—"

"I need an end to this." He waves a hand between us as I slump against the hallway. "I need to cut ties from you."

"I thought we were doing that just fine," I whisper as I run my eye over his perfectly put together outfit.

Fuck, he unfriended me on Facebook the minute we split. I don't even know where he lives now, just that it's in the city, and judging by the threads he's got on, he's doing well for himself.

Of course he doesn't need the money. He's never needed anything from me. Makes sense then, that he wants me to sell to ensure he has no reason to ever see me, let alone talk to me, again.

"If you want closure, Jared, I can get my lawyer to send yours the settlement amount when and *if* I sell in the future. You don't have to deal with me."

He shrugs. "Except I will. You'll still be there in the back of my mind every time I have to list assets, Cam. Or if Kell and I want to apply for another mortgage— the house is still in my name, too."

"So we change it." I push aside the reference he made to the whore who stole him away. "Make a time with the lawyer, and I'll meet you there."

Silence hangs between us, thickening the air in the house—the very reason for this conversation. I push off the wall with the flat of my hand and take a couple of steps toward the lounge room.

"How long?"

He hangs in the entrance hall. "As soon as we can agree on a realtor."

"No." I drop to the edge of the armchair, bracing

myself with both hands on the cushion. "You've got to give me longer."

"Why, Cam?" He ventures as far as the open doorway, ever reluctant to get too close to me. "You've had three years to get what you need out of being here. Staying in the house won't change anything."

"Exactly," I whisper.

I never stayed in the hope it would settle the past, or that the memories the house held could ever ease the pain. I didn't stay to heal. I stayed to keep the wound open and festering, to never forget.

I chose to remain in the home we shared so I would be reminded every day of what I did and why I don't deserve to ever have that kind of love again.

"You need to move on," Jared murmurs as he retraces his steps toward the door. "It's not healthy, Cam."

"I know."

He twists the handle and opens the front door a fraction, resting his shoulder against the edge as he drives the nail home a little harder. "You need to own up to what you did."

TWO

DUKE

"FUCK THIS." WITH THE LID OF THE CAR BOOT propped on my shoulder, I shove the trash in the back out of the way and throw what's left of the driveshaft inside. Why the hell I even agreed to do this for my brother, I don't know.

"Come on, man. It's only a day's drive."

Should have told the fuckhead that if he wanted the car enough, he could have called in to work sick to collect it himself. But no, instead, here I am, big brother, picking up Cody's latest piece-of-shit project that's only going to clutter Mum's backyard some more.

The boot of the HQ Holden slams shut as I let it go, and then round the vehicle to the open driver's door. The shudder started not long after I picked the vehicle up, and then evened out when I hit the open road. I should have known better than to think the car could hold up until I got back, but nope—stubborn old me pushed on in the hope I'd be back in familiar territory before the sun had a chance to rise on a new day.

Day's drive, my arse.

The suspension groans as I drop heavily into the

driver's seat and fish around on the floor for where my phone ended up after it slid off the dash. If the sudden bang and grind wasn't enough to put the shits up me, then the way the fucking car lurched as it lost power was more than enough to send my heart into overdrive. I've had cars break down on me plenty in the past, but I've never been one for surprises—especially not since I got home from my last tour of duty.

My fingers close around the familiar hard case of my phone, and I bring it out from where it's caught under the front edge of the bench seat. The changing hues of the sky tell me I have an hour at most left to figure out what the fuck to do with the immobile vehicle before it gets dark. I don't even know exactly how far I am from the next town; I didn't pay a hell of a lot of attention to the last green road sign I shot past. All I know is that I'm still far enough away from civilisation that the drive-ways are a kilometre apart and the letterboxes are at the required height for rural post.

I swipe through to Cody's number and tap on the entry to dial. Unsurprisingly, he doesn't answer. Which leads me to Plan B: messaging the idiot a picture of the drive shaft in the boot of the car.

"The guy only wants three grand for it—it's a steal," he'd said.

First reason people sell shit cheap: they don't have the time or cash to fix the issues themselves. Nothing's a bargain, not when it comes to cars. You think he'd know that by now, but no. Not my gullible brother.

He flicks a reply through as I drop back into the driver's seat. Probably still at work if he can't answer my goddamn call, yet he can find the time to message.

Typical.

Spare parts?

I drag my hand over my face with a groan, and then tap out a reply.

Yeah, be handy if he gave me some. It's *your* fucking drive shaft, dickhead.

My phone vibrates as a call from his work number comes through.

"Shit, Duke. What the fuck happened?"

"Your excellent buying skills happened, that's what." I sigh out my nose. "Probably had a dodgy universal. You got roadside assistance?"

He chuckles with a snort. "Nah."

Great. "Tell me what the fuck I'm supposed to do with a car that won't drive anywhere, smart arse."

"Get it towed?"

"You spotting me the money?" Paying for it isn't the problem; getting reimbursed if I do, is.

Cody mumbles something unintelligible before answering, "I'll see what I can do. I cleaned my savings out paying for it, bro."

"Course you did." Never the kind to have a backup plan, my brother. "Tell you what," I say on a sigh. "I'll figure out how far away I am from civilisation and see if there's a local garage that can park it up until morning."

"And then what?" he asks.

"And then," I say, dragging out the last word, "we try to get someone to fix the fucking thing."

He hesitates, probably wondering how in the hell he's going to pay for that, or more likely, whether I will. The unexpected chirp of a siren close-by has me shooting up in the seat like a jack-in-the-box to check what's going on. *What the fuck?*

"You can pay me back at a hundred bucks a week. Deal?" I cut the conversation short, eyeballing the cop who's pulled up behind me using my side mirror.

Cody breathes a sigh of relief. "Thanks, bro."

"Thank me when I get the piece-of-shit home. Say hi to Mum for me." I hang up and toss the phone into the passenger's foot well as Officer Holier Than Thou saunters up beside the car.

"Afternoon," I greet, slinging an arm over the back of the bench seat in an effort to pull off the confident and relaxed look.

"Any reason you're parked out here?" He avoids looking at me, choosing instead to run his eyes over the vehicle.

Great. Gym Bro is probably tallying up the bonus he'll get at the end of the month ticketing a run-down car like this. "Had a spot of mechanical trouble, but I'll be off the verge as soon as I find someone to tow it."

"Good luck with that at this time of day." He takes a step back and crosses his arms. It's the human male's equivalent to puffing out his peacock feathers. *Fuckhead.* He probably wants to intimidate me, but all he manages to do is piss me off.

I'm not bothering anyone, not causing trouble. I pulled far enough off the road that I wouldn't be a hazard to other drivers. Why the hell has he decided to pick on me?

"If you could step outside the vehicle for a moment, I'll leave you to get on your way soon enough."

Can I fucking what? "Mind if I ask why?"

His jaw ticks. "Yes, I do mind. Step out please, sir."

Wait until I get my hands on that fucking brother of mine. If I so much as get a warning about anything on this car, so help me God—

"What's wrong with it?" the cop asks as I stand on the grass with my arms folded as well. *Two can play at that game, buddy.*

"Broken driveshaft."

"Hmm." He squats down to shine his torch under the wheel arches, tapping fuck only knows what under there as though a simple knock will confirm its road-worthiness.

"Like I said, I'm trying to jack up a tow. I'll be off the road as soon as I can." In other words, fuck off and leave me in peace.

"I heard you fine the first time." He straightens up, eyeballing me again before he opens the door to check the inside of the car.

"Find anything?" I step forward to try and peer over his shoulder.

He moves backward to get his head out the door, and I leap to the side to avoid any chance of the guy's rear end bumping me. *Not getting that cosy.*

"This what I think it is?" He holds a hash pipe carefully between two fingers.

Fuck my life. You have got to be kidding me.

"Mate, I just picked up the car. It's brand-new, second-hand."

"So you don't know if I'll find anything else in here?"

Sincerely hope not. "Nope. No idea."

"Turn around and face the vehicle, please, and then set your hands on the roof."

"What?" I back up a step, which is *completely* the wrong thing to do.

Gym Bro rests one hand on his tazer, directing me with the other. "Hands on the roof, with your back to me."

Fuck you, Cody. Fuck you.

I do as I'm told, standing in the open doorway as I face the car and slap my hands on the warm roof. The cop closes in behind, squatting as he starts his pat down at my ankles.

I'm totally not okay with this. Not in the slightest.

His hands travel up my legs, and all my unjustified nightmares about being hit on by a guy flash before my eyes. *Totally not homophobic.* Okay, maybe just a little bit. *Let it go, Duke.* He's a cop doing his job. That's all.

A white BMW coupe slows ahead as I breathe deeply in through my nose, and out through my mouth. The setting sun reflects off the windscreen, shielding the driver from my view. I focus on keeping my hands flat on the roof while the cop pats my torso down, watching the vehicle as it turns in a driveway a short stretch up the road, and then stops. The door opens, and what I can only describe as a fucking breath of fresh air steps out to check her mailbox.

Her head turns, the lengths of her dyed silver-grey hair sliding off her shoulder as she looks across the road to where I'm currently being frisked by Officer Handsy. I peer out over my outstretched arm like the creeper I am to check out the young woman's long, leather-clad legs, and slight frame only just hidden from view by a knee-length cardigan that seems to hang from her perfectly. She lifts a hand to shield her eyes from the sun, revealing inked wrists as she checks out what's going down.

"If you could stay where you are while I search the rest of the vehicle," the cop says, moving away.

I draw a deep breath, my feet itching to step the hell away from this car and him. My personal bubble has been violated, and I haven't even got a cigarette to smoke afterward.

"What happens if you find anything, considering the car isn't mine?" I ask.

He sighs, opening the boot to find my story about the busted drive shaft is legit. "You said you just picked up the car?"

I nod, taking the opportunity to look across the road at the hottie again while the cop ducks his head behind the open boot lid. She rubs her arm, as though unsure of what to do, before returning to her car.

"Appreciate if you could keep your eyes off my cousin," the cop warns.

I turn back to find him mere inches from my face. *Jesus ...* "You're a quiet fucker when you want to sneak up on someone, huh?"

"Or maybe you were just distracted." He narrows his steely gaze on me. If this is how the guy reacts when I'm simply watching his cousin, then my guess is the poor bitch is doomed to the single life. Shame, considering she really was a pretty little thing—

"Do we have a problem here?"

"I don't know." I lean a little closer as I frown at the

arsehole. "Do we?"

He steps back suddenly, his hand whipping to his belt as he jerks his chin at my arms. "Hands behind your back."

"What the fuck? This how you treat every guy who looks the wrong way at your cousin?"

"Last chance, or I'll do it for you."

Jesus. This guy ain't playing. I assume the position, laughing at the absurdity of the situation as he wrestles my wrists into cuffs. "Some kind of welcome you've got for your town there, mate."

The air rushes out of my lungs as he crushes my chest to the car, his mouth next to my ear as he grinds out through gritted teeth, "Let's get two things straight: one, you aren't my 'mate', and two, you'll never be welcome here."

Well fuck me.

THREE

CAMMIE

Cars that look like *that* stand out like a sore thumb around here. I check my rear-view again as I pull up to the house, just in case Creepy McCreeperson decides he needs an even *closer* look.

Although with my cousin, Shane, on the case, I can't imagine the guy is going to get far any time soon.

Safe. *For now.* I've got all of an hour or so before I need to turn around and head back out again.

The Friday matinee at the theatre was a hit, all thanks to the Burbank Retirement home renting a couple of mini-vans to bring the residents down for an excursion. It's nice that our drama group has made the weekday matinee a regular for our show season; it gives the older folk a chance to come along when it's quiet, and there aren't as many restless kids they have to contend with.

Unlike tonight. Friday night shows are always the busiest, but isn't that what I love the most? The noise? The distraction? The barely contained chaos?

I drop my kit bag inside the door, checking once more up the driveway for any signs of the old sedan or

Shane. Chances are, the traveller will be gone by the time I've eaten, my cousin having given him the usual once-over and passive-aggressive warning. He doesn't keep getting awards for the town's best cop for no reason. The people of Burbank feel safe as long as Shane's on the beat, and that's all thanks to his take-no-shit attitude.

I stand in the kitchen, staring into the fridge while I decide on what to eat. The rest of the backstage crew get together at the local pub for a meal between the matinee and evening show—a ritual of sorts. Sometimes I join them, but since Jared dropped the bomb about the house on me last week, I've found myself spending more and more time here when I can, absorbing the memories in small, unhealthy doses.

I put myself through the same torturous routine as I do every night, pulling the plastic child's bowl out as I prepare my basic packet meal in the microwave. The matching half-size spoon means it takes me twice as long to eat my pasta, but again, that's okay, because it's all a part of the process.

Of the healing.

Of ripping the wound back open straight after.

Of never forgetting.

I tidy up and restock my kit bag with essentials: water to rehydrate, and snacks for intermission. The sun has set by the time I lock up and make my way back to the car, the dark overtaking the world and trans-forming it into something infinitely more intimate, more mysterious.

My favourite time of day.

I pull the car around and head down the driveway,

glancing to my left as I prepare to pull out onto the road with all intentions of settling my nerves by proving that the beaten-down car has long since left.

Only, it's still there. As is its occupant. Except he's not inside the old Holden anymore—he's seated on the roof. *Odd.*

I should go over and see if he needs help, ask if he's okay. But not only has Shane already been there, done that, but I can tell, even from this distance, that the guy is more than capable of holding his own against the monsters of the night thanks to his jacked size. Anyway, if I muck around with him, I'll be late for pre-show checks, which would involve justifying why to our stage manager. And her wrath is not the kind of attitude I have the time or patience to deal with this week.

Steering right instead, I try my best to act ignorant to the fact the roadside creeper is still there. Yet as I drive up the road, I find myself spending more time looking in the rear-view than I do at where I'm headed.

A fine metaphor for my life.

◆ ◆ ◆

"Jesus, Cammie. You almost didn't make it."

Our sound technician, Bevan, holds the stage door open for me as I stuff my grey cardigan into my bag, leaving me all decked out in black.

"Hey," I say as I dart down the stairs to join the rest of the crew in the first dressing room. "At least it would have given you lot some entertainment, huh?"

With a name like Mary, you might be forgiven for thinking our stage manager is a sweet lady, but there's nothing sweet about her rock-solid five-foot-four stature. With earplugs that could be mistaken for counterweights, and a short, choppy hairstyle that screams "I will fuck you up", she commands the space with nothing short of tyrannical charm.

"Doodles!" she greets, using the nickname she gave me the first time she spotted my extensive ink work. "Glad you could make it back."

Given how I've barely managed to scrape in on time, it was definitely a good thing I didn't head over and check on the random car and driver. "I missed you too much, Mary. Couldn't stay away."

She gives me a sly smirk, and then turns to address the group. Crew members all run through their routines as Mary outlines the same rules as she does every time, adding on performance notes taken from the last show. Our riggers strap their gloves; the lighting technician making scribbled notes on his jotter as Mary gives him pointers about cues that need tightening up. The runners check each other's outfits over, ensuring they're still completely blacked out, our youngest member tucking his green-tipped hair beneath a black knitted beanie.

Satisfied we're all suitably threatened into making sure the show goes off without a hitch, Mary sends us to our stations. I make my way toward front-of-house with Bevan and our other spotlight operator, Susie.

"Kelly came into the pub," Bevan states, his head down. "Probably a good thing you went home for dinner."

"Yeah?" I try to act aloof, but they both know how relieved that near-miss will make me. Small-town gossip doesn't allow for many secrets.

"She said Jared paid you a visit last week," Susie adds. "Seemed real happy about it."

"Bet the bitch did." The three of us round the steps that lead up to the balcony and our stations.

"You haven't seen him in ages, though." Bevan glances across at me.

Rehearsals, especially technical ones when we have to fine-tune our sequences and cues, leave a lot of time for chatting over the headsets. A lot.

"Nope." I pull my gloves and water from my bag, and then tuck it beneath Bevan's sound desk. "He wants me to sell the house."

"What?" Susie tosses her belongings on top of mine, Bevan promptly shunting them all aside with his foot as he takes his seat. "Why didn't you say anything?"

"I was in denial, I guess. Hoped if I didn't talk about it, then it wouldn't happen. He said he wants to cut all ties from me."

Susie frowns, shaking her head. Jared may be her second cousin, but the two of them couldn't be any more different. "He's a right arse, isn't he?"

"I'm not ready to move." I stay focused on my fingerless gloves as I tug them on, one by one. "But I don't think I have any choice."

"Bullshit." Bevan pops his cans over his ears and flicks the power switch to tune in. "You've got options, Cammie. We'll talk about it after, yeah? Mary's doing a mic check."

"Shoot." Susie dashes off to her stand as I make my way behind the last row of seats to mine.

I put my own headset on and flick the power switch

before turning on the spotlight so it can warm up.

"Spot one?" Mary calls through the line in hushed tones.

I glance over at Susie as she wrestles with her cord.

"Spot one?" Mary repeats less enthusiastically.

I flick my mic switch and answer, "She's tangled at the moment."

"Hello, Spot Two."

Susie finally slides her headset on and shrugs across the rows of seats at me. "Did I miss my call?"

"You sure did," Mary replies. "One box to Susie."

The after-party is always a messy affair, and being a not-for-profit, the drama group doesn't like paying for the food and alcohol. They'd rather reinvest any money made into the next production, which is why we have a penalty system. Any infractions during the run of a show incur a payment of a box of beer, or wine. Simple. Knock on wood, I'm still on nothing owed.

"Cam, you on?" our head rigger asks.

"Yeah, I'm here."

"Make it quick, guys," Mary warns.

"Make sure you find me after, Cammie," he says. "The missus has some stuff for you to take to the fundraiser on Wednesday."

"Sure thing."

"What are you wrapped up in this time?" Susie asks.

I slide my gels out to check they're still okay—no spots, or melted patches. "Kindergarten has their disco."

"You still doing that?" Mary adds dryly.

"I am." My light illuminates the wall next to the stage as I slide the cover out to check I'm good to go. Susie's matches mine on the other side. "I have the time spare, so I figure why not?"

A collective groan comes from Susie and Bevan as Mary orders hush over the line. The house lights dip on her cue, signalling five minutes to curtain.

The familiar panic creeps in as the chatter of the audience dies down, the last people rushing to their seats. My gaze roams over the rows, mind-mapping where all the children sit. We've got plans in place should there be an emergency, but even so, the worry within doesn't settle until I know where the children in the audience are and what their closest exit is.

The cue comes through for the house lights to go out entirely, and I position my hands on the grips for the spotlight, turning my focus instead to the welcome burn of the brilliant light encased beside my arm, and the show that unfolds before us.

An hour and a half of bright colours, movement, and rowdy tunes.

An hour and a half where I can pretend I'm anywhere but here.

Anywhere but where she isn't anymore.

FOUR

DUKE

What kind of mechanic's shop closes at three in the afternoon? The only one in town, that's what. Turns out the arsehole cop knew what he was talking about.

The silhouette of the branches above me dance across the stars in the sky as I lie on the roof of the car, weighing my options. I could walk into town—however far that is—and try for a room at some cheap motel. But then that leaves the vehicle out here all night with nobody to watch it, and I know what these country roads are like. It's some scene straight from a *Mad Max* movie: the car enters dusk as one complete unit and remerges at dawn as a stripped former shell of itself.

My brother may be a jerk, but that doesn't mean I need to be one, too. I can at least make sure he gets his investment back in as best shape as I can. Would be a whole lot easier to do if the fucking driveshaft hadn't decided to obliterate on me, but it is what it is.

I already pushed my luck with the cop, only just managing to talk my way back out of the handcuffs. Seems that a few friendly remarks about the current rugby season is enough to sway any red-blooded male around. By the time he released my hands, he'd already mapped out half his fantasy team and was asking me for my picks on the semi-finals.

I got let go with a warning on two conditions: one, I don't eye-fuck his cousin again, and two, the car is off the roadside in the next twenty-four hours. Seems even he isn't so confident it's safe to leave it out here, calling it a "distraction" for bored youth.

Which brings me to the only logical solution: sleep in the car and wait out rescue in the morning.

Fuck my life.

The dark and I don't mix. It's the exact reason why I lie here with the torch on my phone turned on, draining the battery while I do my utmost to pretend I'm not attuned to every creak and scratch of the trees around me.

In my mind, it's not a matter of *if* there's a threat; it's a matter of *where*.

As though my prayers have been heard, the sweeping arc of headlights brings the branches above me to life in an array of lush greens and yellows. I push up on my elbows and spot the hottie's BMW paused at the end of her driveway. The brake lights go out, and the reverse lights come on as she slowly eases back onto the road. I shift around on the roof until I'm seated on the front edge, my legs over the windscreen, and watch as she brings the coupe to a stop nose-to-nose with the HQ. Seems it won't be *my* fault if I'm caught looking at the cousin then, after all.

Without breaking my line of sight from her, I reach behind me and pat around on the steel until I locate my phone and then switch the torch off. Her door opens, and a black boot hits the ground before she completely emerges from the car.

"Hey there," I call out, pressing my phone into my palm until it hurts.

She shuts the car door and steps toward me. "Do you need some help?" Fuck me—the voice is as gorgeous as the woman herself.

"You could say that."

Tingles spread through my hand as I grip the phone to the point of near crushing the case. The guy I picked the car up off? Piece of piss to deal with. And the cop? Easy enough, given the interaction took place in the daylight. But when the moon is dim, concealed behind a bank of lazy clouds? Fuck my night time anxiety.

"Have you broken down?" The woman frowns, walking around the hood to the driver's side. The long cardigan she wears billows around her legs as she moves, her silvery grey hair tucked up in a loose bun beneath a baggy black knitted hat. I narrow my gaze on her, confirming what I thought as the headlights catch the metal—her nose is pierced underneath like a damn bull. *Different.*

"I called the shop in town for a tow, but they were closed." I run my eye over the curve of her arse, the swell of her tits highlighted by the light behind her. "Your cousin helpfully advised I'd have trouble getting a truck that late in the day."

She stops walking as I slide down the windscreen and shuffle across the hood to hop to the ground. "Yeah. Archie has to get his kids from school. Things have been tough since he became a single dad, but he does what he needs to."

"Sounds like a busy man."

"He is." She tips her head to the side, clearly checking me out as her gaze drops to my feet and then climbs back up. "Shane didn't give you too much trouble?"

"That the cop's name?"

"Yeah." She chews on her bottom lip before saying, "He can be a bit intense sometimes."

Understatement. "Nothing I couldn't handle."

"So ..."

"So?"

"You planning on camping out here overnight?"

I grimace and rub a hand over the back of my neck. "Not saying anything bad about your town—"

"But?"

"But I'd rather not leave the car sitting out here in the open all night, so I don't really have much of a choice." I chuckle, nudging the nosecone with my boot. "Even if it is a piece of shit."

"Understood." She brings a hand to her throat as she stares off over my shoulder in thought. My eyes are drawn to the detailed line-work she has there. "Look, I don't normally do this kind of thing for complete strangers, but you're welcome to leave it on my driveway for the night so you can find somewhere better to stay. There's heaps of room to park it in the turning bay."

I twist and gauge the distance to her place. "As great as that sounds, it's a heavy old tank of a car. I might struggle to get it over there."

"So I'll help you push it, get it started, and then I'll

jump in to steer."

I whip my gaze back around and settle on her earnest eyes, rimmed in black. "Are you sure?"

Her arms lift at her sides. "I'm here offering, aren't I?"

"I guess you are." I size her up, estimating whether what little grunt she could add would be worth it or not. "Tell you what, I'll give it a try first while you steer, and if I need your help to push I'll let you know."

"Sure." She doesn't argue the point any further as she marches her heavy boots back to her car, and promptly drops into the driver's seat. Within seconds, she has the coupe backed up at ninety degrees to the HQ so that her headlights illuminate our path.

I pocket my phone and bend down to tighten the laces on my boots. Fucking Cody isn't going to believe a word I say when I tell him about this pretty little Good Samaritan. Might give the arsehole incentive to go out and get his own goddamn car next time, though.

The woman in question passes by, and promptly opens the door of the HQ to take her place behind the wheel. "It's in neutral?"

"Yeah." I step up beside her as she looks around the dash. "The handbrake is just there."

She follows where I point. "Awesome. Let's do this then, muscles."

"Beware," I tell her as I wind down the window. "It doesn't have power-steering."

She smiles up at me as I shut the door. "I kind of figured that." She gives her slender arms a sneaky flex. "I'm stronger than I look."

I hesitate like the creeper I am, lost in the way her

cheeks pinch in as she grins. She's a definite diamond in the rough, a sweet surprise on what's turning out to be a hell of a day.

The grass is already damp underfoot thanks to the cooler temperature now the sun's gone down. My boots slip as I give the HQ its first shunt to get it moving, but thankfully, I don't end up face planting in the dirt, instead putting the car into a decent roll towards the driveway.

By the time we get the vehicle outside her house, I'm jogging behind it, hands braced on the boot, breaths coming short and fast. I let go, watching the car roll as she curves it around to tuck the HQ off to the side of the large gravelled parking bay. Her arms have to be burning with how hard she would have wrenched the steering wheel to get it turned so tight.

"Thanks for this," I call as she steps out of the car. "I'll leave you my number in case you need to get in touch about it before I turn up with the tow truck."

She shuts the door behind her and dusts her palms off on her leggings. "That would be great. I'm sure it'll be fine where it is, though." She steps up before me and offers her hand. "I'm Cammie, by the way."

"Duke." I give her hand a couple of quick pumps, equally disturbed by the fact I broke my personal bubble willingly, and the fact that I liked it.

Her eyes hold mine a fraction too long, and she smiles, small and shy. "You need a lift into town?"

"I don't want to put you out more than I already have." I take the keys she offers, and head for the car to retrieve my overnight bag. "I can walk."

Hopefully the phone battery holds out that long.

"Rubbish," she calls after me. "It's pitch black on that road, Duke." Cammie lifts her hands palms out, eyebrows raised as she wanders over. "Now, I'm not saying anything about my town either, but not everyone's eyesight is what it's cracked up to be. I mean, we've got a few old-timers who live out in these parts, and as much as I hate the fact they do it, I'm also aware they drive home after one too many at the pub or RSA." She reaches the car and props a hip into the side panel while she watches me gather my stuff, her arms folded. "You'd be a hell of a lot safer, and I'd feel a hell of a lot better, if I just dropped you off wherever you're booked for the night."

Girl sure can talk. "I'm not booked anywhere." I heft my bag out and close the boot with my free hand.

"Oh. I'm sure the roadhouse would still have a spare bed if the motel is full. We can ring ahead if you like?"

"Might be a good idea. Don't suppose you know the name of the place so I can look it up?" I dump the bag at my feet and pull my phone out.

Her lips turn upward, the sparkly bullring touching her top one as she does. "I should, I drive past it enough." She sighs. "You know what? Come inside and I'll grab the Yellow Pages."

My next breath catches in my throat as she takes off toward the driveway. Out here, I have options. I'm not caged in by etiquette and social convention. Inside her house, the spotlight's on me if I need to step out. Everything I try to hide creeps that much closer to the surface, dangerously so.

"Hang out at the front door," she calls as she merges into the darkness of the driveway. "I'll go get my car first."

My mouth is dry, my hand gripped tightly to my phone again to bring me back to reality. *She's just being nice. She's not a threat.* I snatch up my bag and head toward her porch as she vanishes from sight, engulfed by the night.

I'm totally fucked.

One social interaction with somebody who genuinely wants to help, and I'm a thousand miles away again, wondering who is really a friend and who is a foe.

Nobody can be trusted—it's a lesson I learnt the hard way.

Especially not myself.

FIVE

CAMMIE

That man has some serious walls stacked up around him. I rub my arms as I head back to the car, partly from the chill of the night, but mostly from the apprehension he causes me.

I've always been the kind of person who can't sit idly by and watch somebody struggle when I'm perfectly able to help. But shit, I think Mum might be right: my empathy will be the death of me.

I can't pick what it is about the guy that makes me wary of him, just that it's not a fear-for-your-life kind of panic. More like I'm waiting for him to destroy me emotionally as a person before he vanishes as quickly as he appeared in our neck of the woods.

I know why I offered to drive him into town. It wasn't purely for his safety. It was because a forty-minute round trip, plus however long it takes to find him a place for the night, gives me the distraction I search for day-in, day-out. Half an hour, an hour. However long it takes to sort out Duke is less time I have to spend lying in the dark, lamenting the silence.

It was never quiet before. I never appreciated that

until all I was left with were the echoes of my thoughts.

He sits on the porch as I bring the Beamer up to my parking spot beside the house. Military-style boots leave me wondering what his history is, why a clearly fit and regimented man sits lost on the porch of a weathered old villa, presumably miles from home.

His dark and cautious gaze tracks me as I walk toward him, turning my keys over in my hand to find the right one.

"Would you like a drink?" I slot the key in the lock and twist. "You're probably thirsty, given how warm it was today. I've got most things in the fridge, so take your pick."

He rises as I push the door open, and just stands there.

I take a step inside as I hold his firm stare. The way he looks at me, it's as though he's waiting on me to work something out for him. *Of course.*

"I'm such a moron," I say with a nervous chuckle. "You've been out there all afternoon; you're probably starving."

He swallows, his chest rising with the deep breath he takes. "Now that you mention it, I am kind of hungry. But I can wait until we get into town."

Something switches behind his gaze, a frustrated rage igniting, yet carefully contained as he steps forward. I move back to let him in, contemplating leaving the door open in case I need a fast exit. Yet as I study the stiff set of his shoulders as he stands in my entryway, bag in hand and back to me, I realise that rage is centred inward; he doesn't mean *me* harm.

Just himself.

Sad.

"I'm afraid that although I can cook, I'm not much of a foodie, so the options are a bit limited." I chuckle as I shut the door, mentally scolding myself for coming across as such a giggly mess. "I can offer packet pasta, a couple of microwave meals, and, if you're lucky, I might have some bacon in the freezer to go with eggs on toast."

His lips curl up a little on one side as he drops his bag. *Was that a smile?* "I'd be happy with dry toast, so whatever you can spare is appreciated."

"Come on," I scoff. "I'm not that Mother Hubbard." I wave him through with me and lead the way to the kitchen.

He takes a seat at one of my two barstools as I busy myself preparing what I'm sure will be killer scrambled eggs.

"So how far did you have left to go?" I ask as I set the pan on the stove.

"You mean, how far am I from home?"

"Yeah." I pull out a stainless-steel bowl and set it down.

"About three hours." He traces a finger across the counter, his eyes glazed as he watches its path.

"Yeah?" I crack the eggs in, adding herbs and salt, and my favourite: dry bacon bits. "North, south, west ..."

"West." He watches my movements as I pour the egg mixture into the pan and stir it around.

"That would place you about ... Greymouth?" I ask.

He nods, spinning on the stool so he faces the counter dead-on. "Just outside of, yeah."

I scrape the wooden spatula along the base of the

pan, mixing it around to get perfect fluffy scrambled eggs. "You're lucky your car made it over here in the first place then." God only knows how he made it up the steep-as-hell viaduct, but I wouldn't be brave enough if I knew the car was on its last legs.

"I didn't bring it over; I only just picked it up," he says. "It's not mine. My brother bought it."

Explains a bit, then.

"If you don't mind me saying, it looks like he got a lemon." I set a plate on the counter. "Hope he didn't pay too much for it. Not that I know what cars are worth, really, but you know."

Duke frowns as I plate the eggs, finishing with a spritz of salt and pepper. The frown remains as I set the plate down before him, quickly adding a knife and fork to the ensemble.

"Shoot. Did you want toast with them?" Why is he so pissed off?

"Nah, it's all good." That twitch of a smile returns as he picks up the fork and pushes the eggs around. "They look great. Thank you."

"No sweat."

I pull a mini Mars Bar from the fridge and lean back against the edge of the counter to eat it while he devours the simple meal I made him. A glimpse of silver flashes at his throat as he leans forward to take a mouthful, and I tilt my head a little to catch it again as he straightens up. The chain is simple; not the kind I'd expect a man to wear, that's for sure.

His shoulders noticeably slope beneath the fabric of his dark navy T-shirt, his bare arms confirming what I guessed the minute I laid eyes on him: he's built. This is a man who carries the discipline to work out regularly, jeans that look as though they're either pressed or usually hung carefully in a wardrobe. He's put together, and yet, he seems so ... messed up.

He rolls his lips together, clearing the last of the taste away as he rises from the barstool. "Thanks, Cammie. That definitely filled a hole."

"You're welcome."

And yet, as I watch him pick the dishes up, rinse them clean and then stack them in the dishwasher I never use, I wonder. What made the *emotional* hole inside this man that leaves him so empty? So lost?

So sad?

SIX

DUKE

EVERYTHING IN HER HOUSE IS EITHER WHITE, OR a shade of grey. It's so light, so deceivingly peaceful. Yet I get the sense this woman projects her clean and crisp image to hide something else.

I wasn't blind to the way she purposefully turned her head and shoulders as she walked down the hall to avoid the pictures on the wall. How she paused and swallowed after she opened the cabinet, and then gently pushed a plastic dinner set aside to get the plate out for me. How her fridge seemed to be stocked with kid-sized juice boxes, yoghurt snack-packs, and the individually wrapped cheese bites you see plastered on a poster in the supermarket with some overly happy kid biting into them.

Details, that I suspect have nothing to do with a small appetite.

"You live here on your own?"

She places her rubbish into the trash, and then hesitates with her hand on the pantry door. "Yeah."

Interesting. "Well"—I check the time on my phone—"it's already after ten, so I guess I better start making some calls before all the motels are done for the night."

"Yeah. I didn't think about that." Her gaze slides somewhere else for a while, and then snaps back to the here and now with scary urgency. "You could just stay here."

"Pardon?" I mean, she's a nice woman and all, pretty, but that's the kind of intimacy I reserve for only my closest friends.

The dead ones.

"I can make up the sofa for you." She shoots out of the kitchen into the adjoining open-plan living room. "It's not the biggest three-seater out there, but if need be I could sleep on it, and you can have my bed. I've got blankets in the hall cupboard, maybe a spare pillow. I can go check if you like, make it comfortable. I mean, you're probably dog tired anyway ..."

I lose focus on her incessant rambling, blinded instead by the crazed focus in her eye as she comes up with a thousand things to keep her occupied by fussing over me. Classic avoidance. Seen it, know it, swore not to embrace the fall-back trait.

And yet, here I stand in the kitchen of a woman who's consumed by it.

"Cammie?"

She keeps talking, even as she disappears into the hallway, her body twisted yet again, and collects a blanket from the linen cupboard.

"Cammie."

She mutters to herself, battling with getting the blanket evenly spread over the sofa.

"Cammie!" Fuck—that's the loudest I've heard myself speak since I got back. I close my eyes and shake away the memories that come with me using my voice to command attention in such a way.

"Oh my God, I'm sorry. I was doing it again, huh?"

"If you mean getting lost in your own little world, yeah."

She looks taken aback by the observation, her lips curling downward at the corners.

"I'm sorry. I just wanted to get your attention."

"Well," she says sharply. "You have it." She slams both hands on her waist, only accentuating how narrow it is and her classic hourglass figure.

"I don't feel comfortable in your bed, or on your couch—even in your house. I don't know you."

Her nose crinkles adorably as she seems to think the problem over. "So let's get to know each other. I don't sleep much anyway."

And there it is: the reason why she's keeping herself busy with my problems.

"Neither."

Her brow softens, the smile returning to her darkly coloured lips. "Well, we've got that in common then. See? We're becoming friends already."

A rare smile pulls my lips apart as she chuckles at her own joke. What is this woman doing to me? I never find reason to smile. At least, not anymore.

"I guess I can make an exception for one night." Even though my head screams no. "Keep your bed; I'll sleep out here."

"So no bestie chat then?" She pouts, mischief in her eyes. "I was looking forward to the popcorn, too."

"Not tonight." I rub my hands across my thighs, fighting the urge to grip something, to tether myself.

"Bathroom's at the back of the house?"

"Yeah. Straight down and second to last door on your right."

"Thanks." I head for my bag, and then pause, turning back to her. "Turn the lights off and take yourself to bed. I'll sort myself out."

"Sure." She glances around, probably unsure if she can trust me.

"Thanks, Cam," I murmur as I turn away and head for the bathroom.

For seeing me.

For helping.

And for not asking questions.

By the time I emerge with brushed teeth, and a healthy few litres of water splashed over my face to snap me the fuck out of this funk, she's in what I guessed was her bedroom when I passed by the open door earlier.

The door is now shut, the gaps around it dark, and all is quiet. *If only her cop cousin could see me now.*

I smirk at the thought and make my way back to the living room using my phone as a torch, grateful she took my hint and went to bed so it didn't seem odd that I would turn another light on when she flicked the others off. Even with the glow beside me, the distinct pitch black that comes from being in the country hits me hard. There are no streetlights, no houses nearby to light up the night, and no cars passing by within view.

The darkness unsettles me, which, for a guy who loved to play hide and seek as a kid, says something. I can't see what's around me—*who's* around me. There's no mental safety map, and no reassurance that I'm okay.

That I'm home. That I'm not *there* anymore.

The way Cammie set the sofa up has my head at the window end—first problem to rectify. I switch the blanket around, and then settle on the cushions with my phone laid on the floor beside me. The low-battery icon flashes up as I lie back and blink up at the ceiling. I reach out and dismiss it; the race is on to get to sleep.

But how can I when all I hear in the darkness are the echoes of the man I used to be?

Coward.

Weak.

Hopeless.

The words I lull myself to sleep with every night. And yet, tonight, they yell louder than ever before, deafening me with their truths.

I can't be this man forever: a guy who relies on the strip of light from a slim piece of technology to hold his nightmares at bay. I can't spend my life checking under the bed, and looking for trouble at every turn.

I just can't.

There's a life on the other side of the canyon of my fears, yet no matter how hard I try, I can't find the bridge to get there.

Which leaves me with only one option: build my own.

Yet I don't know if I can.

SEVEN

CAMMIE

Sunday can't come early enough. Between the show and dealing with Jared's crap about the house, I'm exhausted. My eyes are heavy, my arms sore from holding the spotlight steady, and yet I've got two more shows before I can spend the day doing nothing. I roll to my right, ready to kick things in the guts, and let my gaze fall on the closed door.

Oh, that's right.

I have a guest. Guess that rules out breakfast in my PJs on the couch while I binge on Netflix until show time.

I lie on my side, adjusting the blanket higher over my chilly shoulder, and listen for sounds of life from the other end of the house. Silence is all I get in return.

Maybe he left already?

The display on my phone reads a little after eight. As much of a stranger Duke is to me, he doesn't strike me as the kind to over sleep. Then again, it was well after ten by the time we turned in. Perhaps he needs the rest?

Grow some balls, Cammie. Slip your legs out of bed,

pull on your comfy cardigan, and face the man already.

My legs protest as I shuffle across my room to the built-in robe, and pull my extra-long, extra-thick cardigan off the hanger. Its instant warmth is a comfort, as are the bed socks I wore last night; there's nothing as unforgiving as a cold hardwood floor first thing in the morning.

Well, except Jared.

No light spills from the living area other than the warm yellow hues of the morning sun. Birds sing their praises outside at the warming day as I round the corner and find the two sofas empty. I blink, lift a sleeve-covered hand, and rub my eyes.

It takes me a minute to piece together what's wrong with this picture.

The sofa is stripped of the bedding I left out for him, the cushions barely wrinkled, which indicates he didn't stay there long. Yet what catches my attention most are the feet poking out from where the sofa intersects with its shorter twin.

I shuffle farther into the room and round the three-seater to find Duke propped up with his back jutted into the corner where the two-seater meets the wall. The blanket is tucked under his chin, his hair messed up as he rests his chin on one shoulder.

My feet stay rooted to the spot while I contemplate the best course of action. Do I wake him? Is he the kind to get startled and violent when he wakes suddenly? More importantly, why the fuck is he on the floor like that?

I back away, careful not to disturb him, and retreat toward the kitchen. The electric jug starts its rumble after I flick the switch, my clumsy hands making the two mugs I pull out of the cupboard clang together.

I grit my teeth and set them down as gently as possible on the counter before retrieving the coffee canister from the cupboard. I manage to get a heaped spoonful in the first mug and then make it halfway through doing the second.

"Morning."

I jolt, so sure he was still asleep. Coffee goes everywhere: on the counter, on the floor. I'm pretty sure some skitters across the tiles and under the fridge.

Damn it.

"Morning." I offer a wan smile as I lunge right to wet the dishcloth under the tap.

Duke stands on the opposite side of the breakfast bar, shirtless. I completely miss the stream of water. Pretty sure if I'd been greeted with a full frontal I'd would have forgotten what it is I'm supposed to be doing.

His torso is cut, as in, ripped to all hell. Does this man ever consume fats in his diet? *Holy shit.*

"I spilled the coffee," I verbally vomit.

"I see that." His lazy one-sided grin returns as he lifts his previously concealed hand from behind the counter and reveals a T-shirt, which he then tugs on.

Thank Christ. Not sure my sex-starved libido could have handled much more of that first thing in the morning.

"How do you like it?" *Far out, Cammie.* May as well ask him if he likes to be on top.

His deep brown eyes zero in on my face as I'm sure I turn all shades of red. "Splash of milk, no sugar."

"I took a chance that you were a coffee kind of guy." I wring the cloth out, having successfully found the water, and then drop to my knees to wipe the floor.

It's only when I hear him clear his throat and catch him turn away in my periphery, that I realise what being on all fours does to my pyjama top. *Kill me now.* I slam a hand to my chest to push the loose fabric back over my bare breasts, and rock back on my heels to finish the cleaning job in a more *demure* position.

"Toast?" I squeak out on broken tones.

"That'd be lovely." He rounds the end of the counter and picks up where I left off with the coffees. "You take sugar?"

"One, thanks."

"Sweet enough," Duke mutters as he heads for the fridge to retrieve the milk.

My entire body feels as though it's engulfed in flames as I rinse the cloth out under the cold water. I wring it and set it aside, then dip my wrists under the cool jet for good measure before I switch the tap off. I mean, shit, I knew the guy was cute when I laid eyes on him last night, but nine hours of sleep has attuned my senses somewhat. Last night's eight on the roadside has rocketed to a definite ten. *Or maybe that was the naked torso?* Whatever it was, it doesn't change the fact a smoking-hot guy is casually making me coffee as though he does this every single morning.

"Elixir of the gods," he announces as he hands me my mug.

I take it with a smile, cradling the hot cup as he pops the lids back on the coffee and sugar canisters, and then *pushes them to the back of the counter.*

"That's not where they go."

He cocks an eyebrow as he glances over his shoulder at me. "Really? Where would you put them?"

I set my coffee down and then open the pantry door, pointing to my neat little spot at shoulder height where they line up on the shelf.

"But they're easier to get to on the bench top."

I give him the same look he graced me with, cocking my eyebrow. "But it looks cluttered."

"So?" He frowns.

We stand a moment, squaring off over something as ridiculous as where *my* coffee and sugar should sit. Clearly sensing he won't win this one, the muppet takes his coffee through to the living room, muttering to himself as he leaves.

On the bench top. Pfft. Is the guy crazy? Clean lines. I need clean and clutter-free lines in my house.

My house.

Not that it really is. I groan as I reach for my mug, mentally cataloguing the real estate agents I've looked into so far. Where do I even start when it comes to picking somebody who's going to ensure the best price and not just push for the sale to close out one more deal?

Toast. Right.

"What do you normally have on your toast, Duke?" I call out as I retrieve my toaster from where it's neatly tucked in the cupboard beside the pantry. *Suppose he's going to say he leaves that on the counter, too.*

"Anything," he calls back. "I'm not fussy."

Yeah, only when it comes to how I arrange my kitchen. I roll my eyes at the thought and retrieve the half loaf of bread I have.

By the time my coffee is finished, I have a plate stacked with options for Mr "Not Fussy". Jam, peanut butter, Vegemite, and Nutella.

He turns from where he'd been poised before the French doors, empty mug slung casually from his thumb.

"Hungry?" he teases.

"Thought I better cover all bases." I make sure to hold my pyjama top close to my chest as I bend over and set the plate on the coffee table.

He points to the seven-piece setting in my dining room. "You have a dinner table, you know."

"Exactly. It's a *dinner* table. I never eat breakfast or lunch there." Come to think of it, I hardly eat dinner there either, since it's been just me.

Just me …

"You pick what you'd like first." He takes a seat on the sofa closest to him.

I avert my gaze from his taut boxer-briefs. He could have at least wrangled some pants in the time it took me to make us food. Standing, his T-shirt may cover … certain things, but seated …

"Problem?"

Smug bastard knows there is. "You're half dressed," I say, swirling my fingertip in his direction.

"And you're in your pyjamas still … braless, if I'm not mistaken." *Kill me now.* He leans forward and snags a peanut butter slice, despite telling me to pick first. "So where's the problem?"

I take the one remaining peanut butter and sit opposite. "Are you always this difficult?"

His eyes lose all trace of humour, the slight tilt to his lips diving into a downward curl. "Eat up, Cam."

The fact he picks up on the shortened name those close to me use warms my chest a little. Only a handful of people call me Cam, one of who doesn't deserve that privilege anymore.

"What time is the truck coming?" I ask between bites.

He shrugs, rolling the next slice—Vegemite—into a kind of Swiss roll and shoving it in like a piece of damn sushi.

"Might pay to find out," I say.

"Thought, being a Saturday, the guy might not be at work yet, given he knocked off early yesterday, and all."

"True. Try him after breakfast. Knowing Archie, he'll have his work phone on him anyway."

We sit in silence while he polishes off six slices to my two. His eyes track me as I make my final bites, his gaze unsettling in its intensity as he waits on me to finish and then collects the plate. I lean back on the sofa and eye his wide back as he carries the dish to the kitchen and repeats the same process as last night.

"You know," I call out. "If you hang around for a few more meals, I might actually fill that damn thing enough to use it."

He looks down at the open dishwasher, the plate held steady in his hand. "Do you not?"

"Nope." I chuckle.

"Oh." His brow furrows adorably as he works out what to do.

Keeping the plate in hand, he removes the knife I used to make the toast, and the dishes from last night. I kick my feet up as he searches the cupboards for the dishwashing liquid, loving this domesticated vision, even if it isn't mine to have.

"Woman," he growls. "Where the hell is your dish washing stuff?"

"With the other cleaning supplies in the bottom of the pantry."

He groans, dragging a hand over his face before he shuts the cupboard beneath the sink. As much as I'd love to mess with him some more, I need to get dressed if Archie is going to show up later this morning with the tilt-tray.

"I'm going to run through the shower, okay?"

"Make sure you don't slip," he calls back as I head for the hallway.

"Pardon?"

"You said you were going to *run* through the shower." His head pops around the corner of the wall, that lazy grin back again. "I'd advise against that on wet tiles."

"Smartarse."

I leave the room, smiling like a damn fool as I make my way back to my room to get a change of clothes. My heart thumps painfully hard before racing a mile a minute as I come to a grinding halt in the doorway. With a shaky hand, I reach out and brace it against the doorframe as I realise this stranger in my house made me do something I've struggled to do for years.

I just walked down the hall without twisting away from her face.

And I didn't even have to think about it.

EIGHT

DUKE

Archie turns out to be an absolute bear of a man. I never considered myself to be on the scrawny side, but next to this monster, I feel as delicate as a Victoria's Secret model. His beard alone deserves a medal.

The HQ was loaded easily on his tilt-tray, but not without the guy's clear disdain at having to come out so far to pick it up. I swear he hasn't stopped swearing under his breath since he got here, shooting me filthy looks, and asking how long I plan on sticking around.

The more locals I meet, the more unwelcome I feel.

"I'll make some calls, see how long it'll be to get the part." He slips the weathered baseball cap off and scratches his head with the same hand as he frowns. "Drop by in an hour, and we'll sort out how you're going to pay me. I don't do payment plans, and I don't do cash." He narrows his gaze on me.

"I'm sure we can sort something out." I turn to look for Cammie, finding her fussing over the deadheads on the roses at her front door. "Is that okay, Cam?"

"Huh?" She straightens up, the loose tank she has on

doing nothing to hide her gorgeous figure.

"Archie asked if I could be at the shop in an hour. Would you be able to give me a lift if I spot you some gas money?"

"Yeah, no worries." She dusts her hands off, walking closer. "How are the kids, Archie?"

"Good, thanks, love." Archie's lips split into an enormous grin. *So the guy knows how to smile?* "Dean just started Ripper Rugby, so that's keeping us all busy."

"Awesome. He'll love that."

"They asked after you the other day," the guy says with a wink.

I marvel at the way her mere presence has shifted his entire demeanour. He's gone from brisk and abrupt to relaxed and soft within seconds.

"Well," she says with a shrug, "you just tell me when you'd like a night off and I can come babysit again. I'll bring my popcorn-maker over and the kids and I can have a movie night."

"Sounds great, Cammie." Archie turns to face me as she walks back to her roses, and the smile slides straight from his face, his eyes hard. "See you soon."

"Yeah, thanks." I place a hand to the back of my neck and rub it as he gets in his truck and promptly pulls down the driveway.

"He's okay." Cammie's sudden statement causes me to flinch.

I narrowly avoid throwing a fist at her, keeping my arm stiff at my side. "You shouldn't startle people you don't know like that."

"Oh, come on. I was getting you back for the coffee

incident. You can sneak up on people—why can't I?"

"Because it's not the same," I snap, marching toward the house to get my shit. The sooner she drops me in town the better. I can find somewhere to stay while the car is fixed, get a new phone charger since mine is at home, and put a heck of a lot of distance between this frustrating woman and me.

Cute, but frustrating.

"Hey." She hurries after me. "What was that about?"

"Nothing," I mutter, throwing a hand up to ward her off. "I'll grab my gear and we can go, huh? I've got some other shit I can do until I need to be at the shop."

"We can have coffee," she announces, as though I didn't just snap at her, as though I didn't come close to punching her lights out. "I've got time to kill before the show too. Thought about doing groceries, but we could at least make the trip to town worth it by snagging some of Donna's apple and ginger muffins before they're all gone. Honestly, you have to try them. She slices it, puts a slab of butter in the middle"—Cammie animates the whole process with her hands as she talks—"and heats it up. It's so good." Her voice drops on the last word, her eyes rolling back in her head as her lids droop.

I should find it funny, amusing at least, but her inane ability to talk the hind leg off a donkey drives me nuts. The phrase "silence is golden" was coined for a reason. Pretty sure somebody out there discovered how peaceful it could be when you were left without the chatter of the world, and he decided to aptly name how precious it was to find such solace; he didn't just come up with the saying for shits and giggles.

"I'm sure her muffins are delicious, but you've already done a lot. I wouldn't expect you to waste half your weekend on me."

She frowns, twisting her lips to one side. "Well, if you're sure. I mean, I don't get much opportunity to go there anymore. Work keeps me busy during the week, and between the theatre and the odds and ends I volunteer for, Sundays are pretty much the only time I have to myself outside of errands and she's closed then."

Again with the talking. I pinch the bridge of my nose and sigh. "Whatever, then. Would you like me to give you something for the food last night and this morning?"

She slices a hand through the air with a huff from between her velvet-red lips. "Don't be silly; you were my guest."

The entire fifteen-minute car ride continues in the same fashion. She chats incessantly about pointless shit that stretches from the reason why she chose to have no colours in the house, to why she prefers to listen to old-school grunge rock on Spotify over the modern songs played on the radio. Yet, as I sit quietly in the passenger seat, watching her gesture wildly and crumple her face in a stern expression, it doesn't escape my notice that she avoids the obvious elephant in the coupe: why she's single when clearly, once, she wasn't, and what the hell all the kids stuff around the place is about. Last I checked, young unattached females didn't have entire children's dining sets in their kitchen cupboards, child-sized food items in their fridge, and pictures of toddlers with them in their hall unless they were a mother.

Cammie doesn't once speak like she is. In fact, the only family she makes scarce mention of in her chatter is her parents, who are separated.

It's intriguing, meeting a person who keeps secrets just as I do and viewing it from the other side. I wouldn't know half her struggles if I hadn't been in her house, listened to her talk. Is this how I appear to people I meet?

"Archie's shop is over there." She points out the windscreen at a flat-roofed garage across the inter-section we're currently stopped at. "Your car's probably inside. He doesn't like leaving them out in the yard; thinks people are going to randomly vandalise them." She rolls her eyes as she says this, as though the thought of anybody doing such a thing is too ridiculous to believe.

I eye the place as she pulls around the corner and glides us into a parallel park on the roadside. It seems tidy enough, as though the guy takes pride in his workspace, which is always a bonus when it comes to tradesmen. A messy workshop could mean the same lack of care spilled over into his job, and while I know the HQ isn't some fine supercar, I still expect to be paying for quality work.

"Donna's café is usually packed on a Saturday, so be forewarned that space might be at a premium if you want to eat in." Cammie kills the engine, and removes the keys.

"Takeaway's fine with me." Wide open spaces are also fine with me, so if she wants to eat out in the street, I'm all for it.

She opens her door and rises from the car, promptly reaching between the seat and the door pillar to retrieve her bag from where she'd slung it behind the driver's seat. "Come on," she singsongs when I don't move. "Don't know about you, but that toast has worn off and I'm famished. There's also a tall cup of coffee with my name on it."

I sigh as she closes the door with a thud, and reach for my handle. She needn't worry about me staying in the car too long: the shift in the air as she exited and closed her door was enough to spike my heart rate. There's a reason why I travelled most of the way with the HQ's window down, the same reason why for most of this journey I kept a hand securely gripped to the seat between my legs.

I needed to anchor myself in the storm, find stability to cling to while I ride out the crazy rollercoaster of anxiety I live with now.

Cammie fusses with her hair, smoothing down wayward tresses as she stands on the sidewalk waiting for me to join her. The woman really is a sight for sore eyes. Her skin is flawless, her kissable lips painted a dark shade that pulls my eye to them every time, and those lashes—dark and framing her eyes perfectly. But I don't sense that she spends a lot of time on her appearance—rather she's been doing this look for so long that it's second nature to wrap herself up in the cloak of invisibility before she steps out into the world each day.

You look at her, and she's a pretty girl. She's not a woman hiding a deeper pain. She blinds people with her visual appeal so that they have something to stop at, a reason not to dig any deeper to find satisfaction from being in her presence.

I wonder if distraction is the reason why she's so damn talkative, too.

"I'll pay for this," I tell her as we start toward the café.

"Rubbish." She stares straight ahead, her gaze locked on a real estate office across the street. "I said you don't need to pay me back anything," she protests, but her focus is clearly on that realtor.

"You looking?"

"Huh?" Her eyes burn bright as she snaps back to the present.

"The realtor. You were staring at it. You want to grab our bite to eat and go check out the listings in the window?"

"No," she snaps.

The terse response takes me by surprise.

I hold the door for her, and she hesitates, an apologetic smile pursing her lips. "I'm sorry, Duke. There's just ... stuff going on, and I shouldn't have taken it out on you like that."

"Duck's back." I brush it off with a flick of my chin toward the counter. "Quick, while there's only a couple of people at the till."

She weaves her way through the small round tables—all wooden with mismatched chairs—to the cabinet displaying the baked goods. A couple of people greet her as she passes, and I hang back a few steps so I can watch her interact.

It's curious, the way she clearly knows so many

people in her small community, and yet her home life demonstrates she's probably one of the loneliest people I've ever met.

"Do you have particular tastes?" she asks as we stop at the counter. "Or are you willing to try the apple and ginger?" Cammie nudges me with her elbow, a smile reaching her eyes as she looks up at me.

"Whatever you suggest," I answer.

She goes ahead and orders, remembering how I like my coffee when she picks a flat white for me. Our drinks come in brightly coloured takeaway cups, the muffins individually bagged in brown paper, ready to go. Cammie walks ahead as we leave the café, oblivious to the sneaky stares we get as I follow. I glance back at the people, unassuming types including an older lady with a blue rinse, a white-collared man who stands at the leaner by the front window reading the morning paper, and a mother of twins, who watches us walk out as

she absently talks to one of her children. Nobody's threatening. Nobody seems to offer ill will. Simply people from a town small enough that everybody knows each other's history and habits.

People who look out for one another.

People like I used to be.

Since I've been back in civilian life, I've retreated into my head, building a carefully constructed thick shell around me. The shit that happened overseas affected me worse than I've ever given it credit for. It changed me so significantly that there wasn't much of the old me left inside to recognise the difference.

I'm a completely new guy. And the new guy is a

douche.

"So," I start as Cammie leads us past the car toward the intersection. "You mentioned you spend a lot of time in theatre. Are you a nurse? A doctor?" I swallow back the unease wedging in my throat at being the one to initiate personal conversation. With a woman who gets under my skin, no less. But hey, if I can practice with her, maybe it's the first step towards being the old non-douchey Duke again?

Fingers crossed.

She laughs at my question, handing me the bags of muffins so she can use her free hand to push the pedestrian button. "Not that kind of theatre, although I can see why you thought that with how I said it and all. That's kind of funny actually. I should tell Mum, she'd get a laugh out of it. Me: a doctor. Like that would happen."

Once more with the runaway tongue.

"I meant thespian theatre," she continues. "The drama club in town here do one major show a year, and some smaller street-performance style events in between. I'm part of the crew."

"The crew. Like backstage?"

"Yeah." She flashes me a sweet smile as the walk signal buzzes.

I shake my head in disbelief as we start across the road. If somebody had shown me a picture of Cammie and asked me what I thought her pastime was, I would have stabbed a guess at one of those YouTube makeup bloggers you see chicks sharing all over Facebook.

Acting? Backstage? Never would have picked it.

"Explains the black clothing, I guess."

She drops a short "Ha" before taking a deep breath to prepare for her next verbal marathon. "Not quite. I've always been into that kind of look. I was a Goth in high school, if you can believe it. I guess it sort of spilled over into the rest of my life; but I suppose you could tell that by my house, huh?" She peers up at me as we approach the low timber railings that surround the local parkland. "Although, it's not just my house. I co-own it with my ex, Jared." Her face falls, and I get a sense that *this* is the stuff she said was bothering her before. "He wants me to sell it so we can wrap up our separation."

"I take it you don't want to?" I offer her my hand so she can steady herself as she climbs over the chain linking the bollards.

"No. I love that house. I'd stay there forever if I could. It holds so many special memories, things I don't want to let go of, although ..."

"Although?"

She sighs as she takes a seat at the picnic table tucked beneath a sprawling oak. "He's right about one thing: it's not healthy, the dependency I have on keeping those memories alive."

"The only memory you should ever forget is a bad one." Because, fuck, don't I know that?

"Anderson, Piata! Somebody fucking answer me!"

I shake my head clear and focus on tearing my paper bag perfectly in the centre so I can spread it out to make a kind of plate.

"That's the problem," Cammie says, pulling her muffin out and dumping it on top of her bag, crumbs everywhere. "No matter how good the memories are, they all link into one hell of a bad one."

"And you choose to hang on to it?" I ask as I lean over and take a bite, hoping she'll reveal a little more about what exactly happened to her.

She wasn't wrong, though: these muffins are good shit.

"I feel as though it's the final betrayal if I don't." She tips her head forward, her hair sliding to curtain her face as she picks at the edge of the muffin with her nail. "I've been trying to think of ways to keep the place, ways to make it work. I've been thinking about turning it into a B&B, but I'm not sure if that would be enough separation for him."

I can't be sure what happens in the seconds that follow, only that wherever she goes when the voracious woman finally silences, it seems to absorb all of the negative shit that had begun to surface with her admission about the house. She quietly picks at the food, only the slightest movements made as she brings the crumbs to her lips. A gentle northwest breeze lifts the ends of her hair, giving the sun a chance to catch the lighter tips. She's beautiful, and although I think she knows it, she chooses to ignore it.

"Anyway." The face that lifts to meet me doesn't belong to the same woman. A smile splits her lips despite the fact her eyes are still dead. "Tell me more about you, Duke. What's your story?"

"Not much to say." I shrug, turning the coffee cup in my hand. "I'm between jobs at the moment, kind of deciding where I want my life to go next."

"What did you used to do?"

"Army."

Her eyebrows shoot upwards, a slim finger lifted to point at the chain around my neck. "So *that's* why you wear that. Is that your tags?"

I nod.

"That's so cool."

Fuck—she's just like everyone else. "No," I snap. "No, it's not."

Silence falls between us, and although I can see her fight to keep it that way, she caves and keeps talking. "I didn't mean to piss you off. I've just never met anyone who served before. Thought you might have some cool stories about being overseas, you know, experiences to share, that people like me who've never been in a plane might not have had the chance to have."

"Count yourself lucky, then." I snatch up what's left of the muffin and chew it angrily before swallowing and continuing, "Not all those experiences are great ones, and if I could trade places with somebody who'd never left this great country of ours, I would. But at the same time, I probably wouldn't." I laugh bitterly. "And you know why? Because trading places with somebody would mean they'd have to experience the bullshit I did. I couldn't do that to a person, even if I didn't like them."

"Well, I apologise for being so fucking naïve, then." Cammie bundles her rubbish and rises from the table, marching over to the bin with it. "We'll get your bag out of the car, and then I'll leave you at Archie's."

Fuck. This is why I don't bother with people anymore. She asked an honest question. How was she to know what I went through, why I was medically discharged? And yet, like the douchebag I am, I took it out on her.

Because that's who I am now—a man who blames everybody he meets for bullshit they're not even aware of.

Unless you've been there, you just don't know. And that's not her fault. Hell, it's not even mine. It's nobody's. Yet I just lumped her with it as though she should burden all the blame for the horrors that fucked me up as a man.

"I'm sorry, Cam."

"No." She whips around and marches back to the table, stopping by my side. "That's the second time you've had to apologise to me for losing your temper, and you know what? It makes me think you're not the kind of person I need to be around."

She has a point.

"Let's get my fucking bag then, and be done with it."

"Let's."

I trail behind, my tail firmly tucked between my legs as she marches ahead, struggling over the chain on her own rather than accepting help from me again. Not a word is spoken as we cross the intersection again to her car, which for a chatterbox like Cammie, is kind of poignant.

I can't imagine many people piss her off to the extent that they actually get the silent treatment. And what's weirder is, after wishing she'd shut the fuck up for the better part of a day, I miss her voice.

She pops the trunk on her car, and wrestles my pack out of the back before dropping it unnecessarily hard on the road.

"Thanks for the place to stay." I don't even look at

her; I don't deserve to meet her eyes.

"Best of luck, Duke." She makes no bones about getting in her car and turning it on, signalling that she's ready to leave. I heave the pack up to my shoulder, and after checking the way is clear, cross the road to Archie's workshop.

Her motor runs behind me, the soft hum of the engine as it idles. The urge is too strong as I reach the door to the office, so I give in and look back at where her BMW stays stationary on the roadside. From this angle it's too hard to see what she's doing. The fact she hasn't chosen to drive away yet, to me, means one of two things: she's checking I make it over here okay, or she's too mad to think straight.

Knowing the effect I have on people, I'm going with the latter.

NINE

CAMMIE

Duke swaggers across the road toward Archie's shop. Bets are on the bastard not feeling the slightest bit guilty about his attitude.

I get it—he probably has his demons. But the way he snapped at me, and the hate in his eyes as he did so … That man has one heck of a violent side sitting just below the surface. When and if it decides to show, I know one thing for sure: I don't want to be around to see the aftermath.

I put the car in gear, yet hesitate when my phone rings inside my bag. Returning the shifter to neutral, I race to get my phone out before I lose the call to voicemail. Part of me wonders why I didn't let it go when I see who's calling.

"It's the weekend," I answer, bypassing formalities.

"So?" Jared asks. "What does that matter?"

"I had hoped you'd let me have at least a couple of days off where I didn't have to think about it."

"This is the real world, Cam. You don't get to bury your head in the sand and pretend things don't need to get done."

Arsehole. "What are you calling about then?"

"I've got a shortlist of agents I want you to look at." *I'm still not ready for this.* "I thought if you're home, I'd pop over later and go through it with you."

Fuck, fuck, fuck. I'm not mentally prepared. It's barely been a week since he sprung the decision on me.

Then again—will I ever be ready if the task is something I don't want to do?

"I'm out running errands at the moment, but I should be back by eleven-thirty." I lean forward, resting my forehead on the steering wheel. "I've got to be back on the road by twelve-thirty, though, for the afternoon show.

"You still wasting your time with that?" He sighs, as though *my* social life inconveniences him. "Kell and I are busy right now as well. I can come over between shows, around five."

Of course. Because he won't come now if it means he has to bring *her* with him. He knows better after what happened last time.

"See you then." I disconnect, keeping my head on the steering wheel, and groan. *A goddamn shortlist.* May as well say he's picked the agency. What's the bet the arsehole had the list curated *before* he approached me with the request? I wouldn't put it past him to have a contract drawn up with one of them already, and this is just his fake bullshit show of making me feel "involved".

My eyes drift to the rear-view as I straighten up, but Duke is nowhere to be seen anymore. *Good.* I've had it with men—all of them. The only man I know of that's half-decent is my dad, but even then, he has his days.

I make the drive two blocks down to the grocery

store with my eyes on the road, but my mind is on the past four and a half years.

It wasn't your fault. The same bullshit lie I tell myself every time to try and reason why I should be moving on with my life. But at the end of the day, how can I believe that when I failed the one basic rule you're silently given when you become a parent: keep your child alive.

I pull the keys from the ignition and get out, opening my bag to drop them in after I've locked the car. My eye snags on one of my many crutches, buried deep in the dark recess of the main compartment. My fear morphs into an immovable lump in my throat as I reach in and exchange the car keys for the toy.

A Polly Pocket. One of her favourites, and the very one that would send her into a fit if I didn't have it with me when we went shopping.

Just like I am now.

I should put it back. Hell, I should toss the little plastic compact in the trash on my way past. After all, it's useless to me now.

But it was *hers.*

So instead, Polly takes a ride with me around the supermarket, perched on the fold-out kids seat in the front of the shopping trolley. I pack it away when I get to the checkout, the same sinking feeling taking root in the pit of my gut when I drop the toy back into the dark.

"Hey, Cammie. How was your week? The show doing good?"

I detach from the past and lift my chin to face Ava. She's worked the checkouts at the local grocery store since I was I primary school, always pointing out the chocolate that was on special when I came in with my pocket money. She won't take credit for it, but a lot of the customers come here to keep up with her, rather than save ten dollars shopping on the other side of town.

I'm one of those people.

"The show's going great," I say as I pack the bagged goods into the trolley. "Sold out yesterday's matinee."

"That's good. What one are you doing this time again?"

"*Pirates of Penzance.*"

She chuckles. "Oh. That's always a good one. I should convince Ed he needs to go."

"Call it a date." I throw her a sly wink.

It sends her into fits of laughter as she scans and bags my goods with a speed that belies her sixty-four years. She could have retired a while ago, but I think she secretly enjoys the chance to get paid for catching up with her "children". She's a mother figure to those of us who've stayed local after school finished, always there to lend an ear, or in my case, offer support when it was needed most.

"Saw you with that toy of hers." Ava tips her head toward where my bag sits on the far side of the scanner.

Yeah—she also calls me out on my bullshit.

"I saw it in there when I was putting my keys away," I reason. "I didn't search it out on purpose."

"Maybe not, but why have you still got it in your bag, honey?"

I hold her soft and soothing gaze. "You know why."

She clucks her tongue and rearranges the vegetables so my celery stalks won't tip out of the bag. "A busy woman like you needs more iron in her diet, you know."

"What?" I protest with a chuckle. "I've got lots of vegetables and yoghurt."

"And one tray of meat." She perks an eyebrow. "More iron, miss. If you don't buy it, I'll show up on your damn doorstep after my shift and bring it to you."

"Okay, okay." I hold my hands up. "I'll buy more … next time."

"Good." She totals the order and leans back on her seat while I do the payment. "You showing up for the school fundraiser this week?"

"You know I wouldn't miss it."

Doesn't matter that I have no children at the kindergarten anymore. I owe it to them for the effort they'd put in when I needed the help, to repay the favour.

"Apparently I'm in charge of face painting this year," I tell Ava. "One of the guys on our crew has a son who goes there. He gave me the box of paints the other night and wished me luck."

She chuckles, tearing off my receipt and handing it over. "Girl, if that work of art on your face is anything to go by, you'll be fine."

"It's only a bit of eye shadow and liner, Ava." I tuck the paper into my shopping, purposefully avoiding my bag.

"When you're as old and wrinkly as me, love, you don't bother putting anything on your face anymore, so it's nice to see someone who takes the time to do it right."

"Say hi to Ed for me, and tell him I said he needs to

take you on a date." I leave her with a smile and head out to the car to load up with the groceries.

Archie's tow truck cruises past as I place the last bag into the boot of the BMW, heading away from his shop. I close the car, and watch as he takes a corner and disappears from view. *Guess that meeting didn't take long.* If Duke tried pulling the same attitude he did with me, then I can guarantee Archie would have shut it down just as fast.

My stomach grumbles as I open the car door, making it known Donna's muffin wasn't enough to fill the gap. I mentally catalogue what I bought, planning what I'm going to devour first as I pull out of the car park and head for home.

I make it as far as the edge of town before my food-fantasy is brought to an abrupt halt. I should have taken the long way home for a change, avoided passing the motels on my out. Except I didn't, and yet again, the Good Samaritan inside of me reaches for the handbrake as I come to a stop on the side of the road.

I really need to learn how to mind my business.

TEN

DUKE

"CODY, YOU NEED TO HELP ME WITH THIS."

"I can't. I told you, I've got nothing left after buying the damn thing."

I rest my head in my free hand, hunched over on the side of the highway using my bag as a seat. "Exactly. Which is why I can't trust you to pay me back, either."

He sighs down the line, clicking his fingers in the background—a nervous habit he has when he's thinking hard about something. "I could ask Mum?"

"Like fuck you will. She gave up bailing you out of the shit when you got a job, bro."

The phone call's turning out as to be expected, given the day I'm having. First, I pissed Cammie off, and then, the only place in town that sold the right charger for my phone was fresh out of stock. The one good thing to happen so far was finding out Archie used the same phone, and that he was gracious enough to let me use the charger so I could run the repairs past Cody. A week to get the part couriered in, and then two days to get the job done—and all at the relevant expense for such a big job. Which is a lot.

"What other option do we have?" my brother says with a smug tone. "You gotta get the car fixed so you can get home."

I knew I shouldn't have offered to do this for him. Knew I should have told him to sort his own issues out, and stuck to what's more important—finding a job.

"If I pay for the whole thing, I haven't got enough left to cover the motel, man."

"They have a backpacker's, or something?"

"They've barely got a main street. It's not that big of a town."

He huffs down the line, leaving the conversation hanging while he thinks it over. There's no use; he can't come up with anything I haven't already thought of.

I shift the phone against my ear and straighten up, casing my surroundings as I wait for him to hopefully fold and offer me at least a few hundy to help with the stay. A dark green truck rattles up the road, heading out of town.

"Come on, C," I plead as I shift my bag and myself farther off the road to avoid the truck's backdraft. "Surely you can spare a hundred? Spot me the rest after payday next week?"

He sighs as I drop my stuff down again and look toward the truck as it passes. "I could maybe do fifty." The car tucked behind the trailer unit comes into view.

Shit.

"Duke? Would fifty do?"

Cammie pulls off onto the grass verge.

"Whatever you can spare, bro." I hang up on him mid-sentence, completely over any lame-arse excuse the lazy fucker is giving me, and head toward the little chatterbox emerging from her car.

"Trouble?" she calls, battling with her hair as it refuses to blow anywhere but in her face.

"Not really. I was about to head back into town."

"Town is where I left you," she helpfully points out. "So why are you on the outskirts?"

"Just where I ended up after I enquired at the motel up the road there." More like, needed the chance of bumping into another "friendly" local to be zero to none.

What should have been a simple spot of shopping to get myself a change of clothes, and toiletries, ended up being a grilling.

"What's a nice man like you doing around here?"

"A week's a long stay. You got plans?"

"If you'd like suggestions on what to do while you're here, come back and see me okay?"

God—they're all so damn chipper around these parts. Probably not a big deal to anyone else, but shit, I just want some space to work things through.

"What did Archie say?" Cammie pops her hip as she stands before me, her car idling behind her. If she's left the Beamer running, she doesn't plan to stop for a long chat then. Good.

"That it's fucked, which I knew he'd say, and that it'll take a week to get the parts in, which I hoped he *wouldn't* say."

"Damn. You checked in until it's fixed then?"

I sigh, running a hand through my hair. Still not used to having that shit flapping about on my head in a strong breeze ...

"Look, I appreciate the concern, Cam, but I'm okay.

You can carry on."

Her foot shifts backward as though she's going to take my advice, but then she freezes, the cogs working behind her eyes. "They've got the A&P show this week."

Shit. Fuck local knowledge.

"Where are you staying?" She narrows her darkened eyes on me.

"I've got the option of two nights at the Atlas later in the week, but I haven't found anything until then."

"So your plan would be?" Her hand shifts to her hip.

"Not sure yet."

Her chest rises and falls on a heavy exhale. Of course I look.

"We got off on the wrong foot, I think." *Here it comes.* "If you need somewhere to stay, my place is on the table."

My fist flexes on the strap of my bag. "Never knew it was to begin with."

Cammie swallows, her gaze drifting over my shoulder to the car I hear approaching. "All I ask is that you respect my space and don't ask questions I can't answer."

Her gaze flicks back to me as I nod and offer my hand. "Deal. As long as you can do the same."

She places her palm in mine as her eyes hold mine, and fuck it all if that isn't the game-changer right there. Pressure like I've never known explodes inside my head, ricocheting into my chest before seizing my heart in the devil's chokehold.

I swallow hard as we shake hands, her grip lax before I've even finished the movement. Cammie tucks her hand away as though I've literally burned her with my touch, tucking it beneath the opposite arm.

"Well, I'm glad that's sorted," she says on a chuckle. "Because I've got ice-cream in the back of the car that's probably started to melt, not to mention the milk getting warm and the deli meats … I mean this weather, huh? It's so unusually warm for this time of year …"

I follow her back to the BMW with a smile on my face. She's back to the same chatty girl that got under my skin earlier. Only this time, the irritation doesn't seem so bad.

Perhaps it's the kind of pain that I need to jar me back to being the man I used to be.

ELEVEN

CAMMIE

What the ever-loving hell was I thinking? Since I returned from doing the afternoon show, Duke has not only driven me mad by critiquing where I put my groceries, but tidied my bathroom counter, and made himself at home in the living room with his shoes and belongings spread everywhere.

I check the time on the microwave display again and stare back out the kitchen window that overlooks the driveway. Jared's due at any minute, and even though I've told Duke I've got a visitor and that I'd appreciate him keeping himself scarce for it, Jared's not one to let a detail like a houseguest go without interrogation.

The polished black paintwork of Jared's truck comes into view in the clearing between the trees. I pull a levelling breath as the vehicle approaches the house, and promptly parks in such a way as to block the driveway for anyone else. *Typical Jared.*

"That your guest?" Duke asks from my right.

I glance over to find him at the window beside the dining table, eyeballing the truck. "Yeah."

He simply nods and backs away. "I'll be out in the

yard. Come get me when you're done."

"Thank you."

He brushes it off with a flick of his hand as he heads for the hallway. The sound of Jared's car door slamming shut sends me into a frenzy. I whip about the living room in a blur as I pick up any evidence of Duke I can find, and set his bag, shoes, and jacket in the corner, tucked behind the largest sofa. Hopefully, Jared will be so damn distracted with his own agenda, he won't notice.

The echo of his knock on the front door jolts me out of my panic. I head into the entry, and suck another, less satisfying, deep breath as I reach for the handle to let him in. "Right on time."

The arrogant bastard breezes past, a white portfolio tucked under one arm. "There's something to be said for punctuality, Cam. You should try it."

Arsehole.

"Make yourself at home," I quip as he takes a seat on the sofa and spreads his papers out over the coffee table.

Ice-grey eyes meet my own. "I will, thanks, considering it's still my home, too."

I press my lips together and retreat into the kitchen to avoid saying something that really isn't going to help my plight. With a crisp carton of juice in my hands, I return to take a seat opposite Jared, on the floor, and pop the straw into the foil-sealed hole.

"Fuck me, Cam." He rolls his damn eyes at me. "You still drink those?"

I stare down at the carton in my hands, realising that I grabbed it without a second thought of how it looks.

"I'm only one woman. A whole two-litre bottle takes me too long to get through."

My lie convinces him no more than it does myself. We both know why I still drink from kids juice boxes.

Because I can't let go.

"What are the choices?" I ask, doing my damnedest to divert the subject.

"Terry Searle, Bob Anderson, and a woman—Amanda."

I close my eyes briefly, reopening them on the wall rather than looking at the man opposite me. Good to see some things never change; he still feels women are to be looked at and appreciated at face value, rather than used for their skills in the business world.

"Tell me about the *woman*."

His jaw clenches. "She's fresh on the job. You wouldn't want her."

"And yet, you brought her info along to show me." I cock my head to the side and narrow my gaze on him. "Why?"

"She's Kell's step-sister."

Bingo.

"Obligation is a bitch, isn't it?"

I'm getting to him; I can tell. His hands track a path up and down his chino-clad thighs, his jaw firm as the tell-tale vein in his temple swells. *Easy on, Cam.* If I want a chance at him agreeing to my proposition, then I need to tamp back the attitude.

"I've heard of Bob," I appease. "What's the Terry guy like in your opinion?"

Jared drivels on for the next however long about this guy's ranking in his company, the last few sales, and why he thinks that Terry is the man who can secure us a good price. Correction: secure *Jared* a good enough price. No amount would make me part with this property if I had final say in it.

It's my home.

It's where I left my heart, and I'm yet to get it back. I can't go yet.

"Are you even listening?"

"Pardon?"

Jared eyes me cautiously. "You've got that faraway look."

"I was listening."

"But?" He laces his fingers, his elbows resting on his knees.

"But, I've been thinking the past few days, and what if we didn't have to sell to separate completely?"

He frowns, thumbing his chin. "I don't follow."

"You don't care about the money, right?"

"Not particularly, although I have plans for what I could do with it." His frown deepens.

"What if I turned the place into a B&B, and the business paid you back what you invested over the course of the next five, ten years?"

"That's a long loan, Cam."

"I could even apply to the bank for it."

"A mortgage on a mortgage?"

"A business loan." I set my empty juice box down.

He sighs, pinching his nose with closed eyes as though I'm some child he can't make head or tails of. "Two problems, Cam." I feel scolded the second his eyes reopen on me with the tired frustration that I came to know well during our last few months living together.

"One, I'd still know the money came from you, so that doesn't really work as far as cutting ties completely."

"Selling this house won't erase who you were or what we had once," I remind him.

"Two," he snaps, frowning at my interruption. "I don't think the bank would loan you *that* sum of money on the promise of a few stray vagabonds stopping through every so often. You'd need a solid business plan to convince them it would turn enough profit to cover the investment, and I'm sorry, but a cute villa in the middle of nowhere doesn't really fit the bill."

Fuck him and his concrete boots made for stomping on my dreams. I honestly thought it was a solid plan. Look at the popularity of sites like Airbnb. People jump at the chance for a weekend away in a quiet oasis.

He takes my silence as acceptance, and slides the realtor profiles across the table toward me. "Pick one, Cam."

Naturally, I point to the woman. "Her."

He slumps back in the seat in true dramatic Jared style. "Really?"

I nod.

"I'll call Terry in the morning." He bunches the papers up, ready to leave.

"No. You'll call Amanda."

His glare is enough to strip paint. "Terry."

"Damn it, Jared." I push violently to my feet, my hands fisted at my sides. "It's my house, more than yours. I own the majority share of it, and I say pick Amanda. You don't get to tell me what to do anymore. You gave up that right when you checked out of your responsibilities as a husband." A tear tracks over my cheek, but I refuse to wipe it away. Let him see the damage he'd caused. Let him see what he does in the vain hope that somewhere in that cold heart of his it still beats red.

"*I* checked out?" he roars, stamping a fist to his chest. "Well, shit, Cam. I was simply following suit, since you'd long checked out of being a *mother.*"

"Get out." My jaw aches from the pressure. "Get the fuck out of this house!"

He snatches the file with a flourish and storms from the room as my carefully contained guilt crashes forth over the walls of my denial in a tidal surge that the greatest engineer couldn't have withheld.

I never checked out from my responsibilities as a mother. I might have failed our daughter, but fuck it all, I *never* stopped being her mamma. I loved her until that last breath, even as my own threatened never to come again. I still love her, and damn it, I'm still her mother. The love for a child doesn't disappear after death. Some days, I believe it simply intensifies, until the ache of what is lost is all you can feel, hear, and taste.

My hand shakes so violently I can't even hold my phone, let alone trust myself to tap my mother's number to dial. All I want is to talk to somebody who I know will understand, someone who'll have my back after that showdown. I need validation that Jared *is* being unfair, and that I have every right to fight to stay in the house that acts as a shrine to my greatest mistake.

"You okay?"

The whispered question takes me by surprise. I never heard Duke come back inside. I'd totally forgotten he was here.

"Not really." I offer a pathetic smile as I sniff and wipe away my tears.

"Want to talk about it?" He crouches down beside where I've crumpled onto the sofa.

"Not right now." He frowns as I pat his knee twice and push to my feet. "How about we decide what we're having for dinner tonight? I don't think scrambled eggs will cut it two nights in a row, huh?"

He watches as I absently wander through to the kitchen, confusion clear in his richly coloured eyes. "You know"—his lazy grin returns—"there is more than one way to cook an egg."

I can't hold it back—I laugh at his ridiculous comeback. "Yeah?"

"Poached, fried, hard-boiled. I could get real fancy and do a platter with the whole lot assorted on it." He follows to where I am, taking a seat at the counter same as last night.

"As appealing as that sounds, we need to have a proper meal. It's a grocery day ritual. Tell me you do it, too."

"Do what?" He rests his elbows on the counter, which only serves to showcase how broad his shoulders are.

"Make the most of having fresh food and whip up a healthy feast."

Duke shakes his head. "Afraid not. I'll let you in on a secret."

I lean in conspiratorially. "Tell me."

He matches me, leaning over the counter as far as he can manage, to whisper, "I'm a lousy cook."

"Well," I announce, bouncing on the balls of my feet, "you've come to the right place, my friend. Because although I don't have much in my cupboards usually, that doesn't mean I don't know how to whip up a feast." I tug a wooden spoon from the drawer and point it at him. "Settle in, and watch a master at work."

TWELVE

DUKE

SWEAR TO GOD, I HAVE NEVER EATEN SAVOURY meatballs as good as the ones Cammie makes. They're nestled on a bed of rice that she made even better with a secret mix of herbs and spices, and drizzled with homemade sauce. She wasn't kidding when she said she was a master in the kitchen.

Her eyes are alight as I sop up the last of the sauce with a slice of bread. "Good?"

"Woman, you could cook for me any day."

Her smile fades, the light in her eyes extinguishing. "I miss making these kinds of meals; I don't get much opportunity to anymore. No point making such a huge dish for just me."

"Well, I'm in town for at least a week, so I'm telling you now, make the most of it. I won't complain." I throw her a wink, just to round the playful tone I'm going for off.

It works, her features softening as she straightens in her seat and reaches for my empty plate. "You know, I might just take you up on that. I've got one rule, though."

"What's that?"

"The person who cooks doesn't have to do the dishes." Her lips tilt up on one side as she stands, and then carries the plates and utensils to the kitchen.

"Fair enough." Hell, if a little grunt work is all I have to do to get a cooked meal like that every night, then have at it. "I'm guessing you're back to work Monday?"

She nods, putting some of the ingredients she'd left on the counter away in the fridge. "Yeah."

"You okay with me hanging here while you're away?" It'll make me feel better if there is somebody here to watch the place. I didn't catch all of what she said to that jackass who came to visit this afternoon, but I get the vibe he's some jilted ex. And that never fares well.

"I don't mind." Cammie returns to her seat at the table, a bottle of water in hand. "Oh. I'm sorry. Did you want one?"

"No, you're fine."

She nods, unscrewing the cap. "What do you think you'll do to pass the time? I've got Sky TV and a Netflix subscription you're welcome to use."

"Don't really watch much TV." Something about having to sit still for that long without it being productive time spent doesn't fare well with me. Never has.

"You're kidding." Her jaw drops as she openly gapes at me. "You don't do movie marathons? Binge-watch an entire series?"

I shake my head.

"Duke, you don't know what you're missing out on."

I've got a fair idea. "Rather be doing something

constructive with my hands."

She leans back in her seat, looking me over me as though I'm some interesting specimen on display at a zoo. "What do you do then? To pass the time?"

"Fix things. Re-sell them. Try to make a little extra to get me through week to week."

Her expression grows serious, the smile lines around her eyes fading as the corners of her mouth turn down. "I know you don't like talking about the army, but do you mind if I ask, do you get paid anything after you leave? Like, I've heard you get a kind of pension from them, but I don't know if that's just older vets who get it, or if you had to have a certain rank or something."

"You get something. But it's not enough to live on."

"The government would help, right?"

I shake my head. "Not unless you fall into their regular benefit categories: sickness, unemployment, that kind of thing."

"And I take it you don't?" She taps her fingers across her bottom lip, drawing my attention there.

"Only been out of work for a couple of weeks, so I don't qualify for help yet, no." Not that I'd take it. I've never felt right about accepting a hand up when I should be able to do it myself.

I drag my gaze from her mouth, and find her watching me. Her eyes are lazy, her fingers stilled on her bottom lip as she absently pushes at the plump flesh.

Fuck. This woman ... She's got no idea what she's doing to me right now. Absolutely none.

"Anything I can do around here for you to say thanks

for the board?" I shift in my seat, doing my best to subtly rearrange my jeans so the fabric doesn't choke my dick so hard.

"I'll think on it."

For once, the woman appears out of things to say. Is that because of me? I test the theory, leaning back in the seat to stretch my arms, lacing my hands behind my head in a way I know shows off my muscles.

The hand over her mouth drifts to her throat before she snaps out of the trance with a gasp. "Tell you what ..." She comes close to tripping over her chair in her hurry to stand, "you wash, I'll dry. A bit of teamwork to cut the chore in half, huh? I've got less than an hour left before I have to be back at the theatre anyway, so the quicker we do this the better."

Interesting.

I give my arms a flex before dropping them to my sides and rising to my feet. I'd say something further, rile her up a little more, but she's already in the kitchen with her head in the pantry as she retrieves her cleaning supplies from the cockamamie place she keeps them.

"I really don't get why you don't keep them close to the sink, you know, where you use the dishwashing liquid all the time."

She stills, bent double with that pert little arse poking out toward me. "Really, Duke?" I shift my gaze up her body to her face as she straightens and turns toward me. "Less than twenty-four hours in this house, and I've already lost count of how many times you've criticised the way I keep it."

"Observation, is all."

She dumps the liquid and dishcloth beside the sink, and turns to me, one hand propped on the edge of the counter. "You know, most people have this thing called a filter. It stops them saying stuff that isn't crucial to the succession of the day, snide little remarks about things that don't matter like, oh I don't know"—she taps a finger against her lips—"where somebody keeps their dish washing liquid."

I lift both hands, walking toward her. "Just trying to make your life easier, is all."

"Appreciated, but it's really not necessary." She steps aside, giving me clearance to set up.

"When is the next show after tonight?" I ask, feeling a change of topic is in order while I wait for the water to run warm.

"Thursday. We only do five a week: Thursday night, two on Friday, and two on Saturday. It amazes me we can manage to pack most of the shows out, considering there aren't that many people around here." She chuckles. "But I guess we all like a little escape, right?"

"Yeah." I dump a healthy dose of liquid into the water and swirl it around to create bubbles. "I guess."

Except when I escape reality, it's to a place infinitely more horrible. The kind of landscape that nightmares and horrors are made in.

The kind of landscape that once wasn't simply a bad dream.

It was my reality—my every day.

My life.

THIRTEEN

Mariana Harwood ran a hand through her long brown hair and sighed. Six weeks of doing this dance, and it never got any easier. Her fingers snagged in a knot, the brittle ends of her hair reminding her how long it had been since she took a day to look after herself.

Yet she wouldn't begrudge the reason she hadn't. Her children were her life, especially after her husband of fifteen years had up and walked out when the kids were still young. Oftentimes, their hugs and whispered words were the only thing that held her together on the toughest days.

Which is why it was only fitting she returned the favour and did everything in her power as a mother to soothe the pain her oldest son was in.

"They let me know that you're being discharged next week."

Her baby boy—not that he was much of a baby, or a boy anymore—rolled his head to face her. "Yeah. They said."

"How do you feel about that, Duke?"

He didn't reply. He simply shut his eyes and rolled

his head to the face away once more.

She had thought receiving the phone call about his injury was the hardest moment in her life. But she'd been wrong. Having somebody tell you in a clinical baritone that your child would be returning home on a medical flight caused pain, sure. But nothing wounded her as deeply as the cold distance that accompanied Duke when they wheeled her boy off that plane.

Gone was the laughing joker she would curse out as he sprung another prank on her while she tried to organise dinner for the family. Gone was a boy she remembered giving his little brother grief because at four years old, Cody didn't quite have the same level of coordination to jump his BMX as Duke did.

No. Instead, the army returned a shell of a man to her. One who sounded like his father: bitter and jaded. One who looked like the boy she loved, but acted nothing like the Duke she'd held tight when he'd broken the news to her that his turn to deploy had come.

"I thought perhaps we could take some walks on the beach. Ease you into regular exercise again."

His chest heaved with a sigh, the hospital sheet doing nothing to disguise the steel rods that they had inserted into his leg to keep the femur steady while his skin healed enough to withstand surgery.

"Let's get through one day at a time, okay, Mum?"

"Okay." Mariana reached out and took her son's hand, offering comfort the only way she knew how. Her words didn't matter to him anymore, her actions redundant when he showed no interest in the special arrangements she'd made so his recovery at home would be as pleasant as possible.

No. The only thing that still got through to her boy, that still made his breathing slow and his lips lose the permanent scowl, was her touch.

The simple tune slipped from her lips without a second thought as Mariana hummed the notes to "Somewhere Over the Rainbow". She tore her gaze from the turning leaves on the oaks outside and smiled as her son's brow smoothed, and his lips twitched in and out of a smile—minute, but enough that a mother could still tell.

Recovery had just begun, but in her heart she knew that all she had to do was hold tight and everything would be okay.

One day, *her* Duke would come home.

FOURTEEN

DUKE

War wages within me as I stand in the middle of Cammie's living room, my elbow propped in my hand while I rub my fingers over the growing stubble on my jaw.

She said to kick back, relax, and do nothing while she was at work. But this woman knows nothing about me, and if she did, she'd realise how ludicrous that sort of suggestion was.

Idle hands are the devil's workshop.

Her décor is simple, understated. Yet, the longer I've spent with her, the more I've come to know one crucial thing about Cammie: she's no more of a neat freak than I am a social butterfly.

She hides her shit well, literally *and* metaphorically. Open her cupboards and you're greeted with piles of seemingly useless junk, hoarded and treasured, yet not precious enough to be on display or utilised. Open her mind and I'm sure you'd find the same, a mess of a woman who can't let go of things that hold no purpose anymore.

I shouldn't. She'll flip a switch if I do, but the thought of sitting around watching television all day has me looking for the nearest bridge to jump off.

Just a little—she won't mind too much.

I delay the inevitable by heading to the fridge and pulling out a Pop Top bottle filled with apple and blackcurrant juice. Sipping the sweet drink, I wander through the living room to the hall, figuring I may as well take the opportunity to venture farther than the three rooms she's already shared with me. Maybe then I'll find something to do, some task I can keep occupied with that'll help her out, show my thanks for her hospitality?

There was something panicked behind her eyes when she left for work this morning. *"Help yourself to anything in the kitchen. Chill out in front of the TV. Maybe go for a walk."* Almost as though she was trying to direct me.

She seemed determined to give me suggestions on how to fill my time, to the point where it's reignited my curiosity about how exactly this woman came to be living on her own, save for a closet full of child-size skeletons and ghosts.

The last of the drink slurps through the Pop Top with a loud gurgle as I veer left in the hallway and head toward the bedrooms. Cammie's is the one on the left, adjacent to the living room. I figured that out the first night.

Her door is open just a crack, not quite enough to see what's on the other side, but enough that I get the idea her room is decorated much like the rest of the house: void of colour.

Pulsing the empty drink bottle in my hand, I

concentrate on the crackle of the plastic as I crush the container in, let it out, and repeat. The sound grounds me, bringing my fledgling paranoia into check as I stand outside her door, wondering where to go next.

Cammie doesn't strike me as the type to take advantage of another person, but the walls she holds around her definitely set me on edge. People who avoid the truth are those who are afraid of what reality will bring.

I know. I deflect and redirect with the best of them, steering conversation away from anything that skims too close to the heart of who I am.

I head toward the room at the front of the house. It's closed off; the heavy timber door is stained an ominous dark walnut. To the left is the spare room, completely empty save for a dozen or so packed boxes of odds and ends. Past that is the bathroom, and then the laundry and toilet. I mentally map the house in my mind.

The front room has to be another bedroom.

Walk away, Duke.

My hand burns to open that door. Fuck, does it burn. But she's shut the room off for a reason, and if there was a spare bed in there I'm sure I would have seen her open it before now.

I make my way back through to the kitchen to bin the empty juice bottle. The lid on the trashcan rings out as it slams shut, yet my focus is on the car that makes its way up the driveway.

Late model coupe. Yellow. *Probably female then.* Clean and basic. No modifications, as though it's just rolled off the factory line. *Older person.*

The occupant gets out as I open the front door to

greet whoever has come to visit. A short woman with silvery hair pulled back into a high ponytail steps toward me, a smile lighting her face.

"You must be Duke." She holds her arms out as she closes in for the kill.

I go stiff as a rod as she clamps both hands down on my biceps and leans in to place a chaste kiss to my cheek.

Get off … get off … get off …

"I'm Clara." She backs up a step, giving me room to breathe again. "Cammie's mum."

One look in those familiar eyes and I know she speaks the truth. "Nice to meet you."

Clara runs her eye over me while I stand there, hands jammed in pockets, not sure what she wants me to do next. Do I invite her in? It seems odd given she's probably been here a thousand times more than I have.

"I won't stay long." Her blue eyes snap back to mine as her smile widens once more. "Cammie just asked that I pop over on my way into town to see if you needed anything. She said you don't have a car at the moment."

"I think I'm okay." Her long flowing cardigan, leggings, and tall boots remind me so much of her daughter. "Would you like to come in?" Seems the only polite thing to do.

"That would be lovely." Clara claps her hands together and heads for the door. "I'm dying for a hit of caffeine."

Her ears hold small gauge plugs, a tattoo peeking out from the collar of her shirt at the back. She's eccentric in her style, definitely not confined to the "normal" standards most women her age are.

I like it.

"Tell you what," she calls over her shoulder as she breezes through to the kitchen. "I'll make the drinks. You do me a favour and see what biscuits my daughter has in her pantry."

"Yes, ma'am." I close the front door behind us and pull in a deep breath before joining her.

Nothing to worry about. Sure, she's the fifth new person I've had to deal one-on-one with in as many days, but shoot, she's no more of a threat to me than her daughter.

I've got to stop panicking at everyone and everything. I need to trust.

Just trust …

Clara gives me another warm smile as I round the corner to the kitchen, the coffee canister already laid out on the counter before her. Clearly she knows the quirky places her daughter keeps things.

"Knowing Cam," she says with the lilt of a laugh, "she'll have some Tiny Teddies or other childlike rubbish. Have a dig on the top shelf, to your left. She might have something better up there collecting dust."

I locate the biscuit tin on the middle shelf, and sure enough, it's filled with Mini Bites, coated in pink icing and sprinkles. The search for something else comes up empty, so I pull out one of Cammie's plastic princess plates and set the pink-iced biscuits out on it.

Nobody can know I did this. May as well pack up my balls and hand those over, too.

A chuckle escapes Clara as she looks between the plate and my mortified face. "Oh, stop it. It's not as though all that pink is going to suck the testosterone right out of you now, is it?"

Can she be sure? "Good thing I'm hungry, huh?"

Her eyes crinkle at the corners before she bursts out laughing, shaking her head as she turns back to the mugs of coffee. "How do you have it?"

"White with none, thanks."

Clara finishes the drinks in silence as I set the plate down on the counter and take a seat on one of the bar stools. She brings the steaming mugs over and sets them down beside the plate, choosing to remain on the opposite side of the counter from me rather than take the other stool. Her necklace rattles as she leans forward and props both elbows on the surface, resting her chin on one hand. "So your car's broken, huh?"

I peer across at her over the rim of my mug. "Cammie's filled you in then?"

"A little." Her lips curl with mischief. "What do you do for a job, Duke?"

She didn't tell her that much, then. "I don't have one at the moment, just a hobby that keeps me busy."

"What did you do before, then?" She reaches out and snags a tiny biscuit, popping it delicately into her mouth.

"Labourer. But it didn't work out." I take two biscuits at a time to at least pretend I'm eating something a bit more satisfying.

"Oh." Clara's eyebrows lift as she takes a casual sip of her coffee. "Cam said you were in the army."

"A little", my arse.

"That's right."

"Medically discharged?" Her eyes narrow in on me,

the light and airy nature of her voice sinking to something more take-no-shit like.

I nod.

"Well"—she straightens—"I'm sorry to hear that."

Not as sorry as I was to do it.

Her gaze drifts to the living room, and to the spare blanket folded on the arm of the sofa. "Don't tell me she has you sleeping on the couch."

"It's fine, honestly. I'm thankful for the help." For some reason, I feel as though I need to defend the situation. I guess it's the tone Clara took when she made the statement, much like one my own mother used when she was mad at some ridiculous idea Cody and I had decided to execute without proper consideration for the consequences.

"No." She shakes her head, coffee poised halfway to her lips. "You tell that daughter of mine that a couch is no place for a fully-grown man like you to be sleeping."

"She did offer to swap, to let me have her bed and she'd take the sofa," I explain. "But I said no. Honestly, it's fine."

"It's not." She snorts. "She has a spare bed; she can use it."

"Does she?" *The closed door.* I was right.

"Yes, she does." Clara takes a sip, her eyes hard as they stay connected to mine. "She simply *chooses* not to use it."

I stare down at the mug between my hands, wondering what exactly I've stumbled into here. More so, why I care. I could heed the warning and stay out of it, sleep on the sofa and not say a damn thing to Cammie about what her mum has to say. I could fly below the radar and bide my time until the HQ is fixed and I'm on my way.

But I can't get the trail of clues out of my head: the plastic dinner set, the food, the closed off room, the pictures she avoids at all costs … the ex.

This girl's dealing with something greater than what she can control, and I want to know if I'm right in thinking what. I want to know if anything I can say, I can do, can help ease the burden she carries.

Clara sighs, setting her empty mug in the sink. "I take it by the look on your face she hasn't explained much about her situation to you."

"Not really." I push my drink aside. "But then, is it my business?"

She shrugs. "I guess not. But at the same time, somebody neutral might be the ear she needs." Her gaze drifts out the window, her brow furrowed. "She doesn't talk to us about it: her father, me, her friends …" Her head drops as she sighs. "She needs to talk to someone."

There's no way out of this. I accepted Cammie's offer to help thinking her life out here was peaceful, uncomplicated. But I see it now. This house is her oasis, a clearing in the middle of a raging forest fire.

"What happened, Clara?"

She swings her head my way, her hands braced on the edge of the sink. "I can see you're a smart man, Duke." A sad smile graces her lips. "I'm sure you can work it out."

FIFTEEN

CAMMIE

"Everything's fine, love." My mother's voice echoes around the confines of my car. "When I left this morning, he was thinking of taking a walk. He seems trustworthy."

"He didn't get abrupt or anything?"

I sent Mum around to case Duke out for me while I was at work. Not that I don't trust him, exactly. Simply that I wasn't *sure* of my ability to judge a person after the way he flipped out at the park and then acted as sweet as pie last night.

"He was perfectly lovely," Mum says with a little too much enthusiasm. "Not a bad-looking man, if I do say so myself."

"Eww, Mum. He's young enough to be your son."

"So?"

I shiver, bracing my hands on the steering wheel a little tighter. I do *not* need to know about that part of my mother's life.

Ever.

"Why are you making such a strapping young man sleep on the couch, Cam?"

I grit my teeth at her question. She damn well knows why.

"It can't be good on his body to be cramped up like that," she presses. "He'll end up with a crook back by the time he leaves."

"He doesn't sleep on the sofa, Mum," I clip out. "He sleeps on the damn floor, so if he gets a bad back, that's his problem."

"On the floor?"

"Uh-huh." I slow the car and turn into the drive. "I'm home now, though, so I'll talk to you later, okay?"

"Sure thing."

"Thanks, Mum."

"Love you, Cam."

I press the red button and end her call as I glide to a stop in my parking spot. She wants me to put him up in the second bedroom. Is she insane? Why would I let him in there to ... to *move* things and sully the place with his smell, his presence? Why would I do that?

My head pounds, and my hands still ache at the coiled rage over it all when I step out of the BMW and head for the house. I barely make it two steps before I veer off course and walking toward the strip of lawn that runs down the side of the house, out to the driveway. *What the hell?*

The edges are trimmed, the lawn clipped in perfect lines like you'd see at some fancy estate. Curiosity gets the better of me, and I continue down the side of the house toward the back. Sure enough, the whole rear lawn has been clipped in the same fashion: one light green stripe, followed by a darker one. Stripes that make the quarter-acre seem twice the size. He's even gone so far as to remove some of the stubborn creeper vines off the fences that separate the yard from the paddocks beyond.

"Did I do a good job?"

"Holy shit!" I cry, a hand clasped to my chest as I turn to face him. "You need a goddamn cow bell or something."

"Says the woman who scared the bejesus out of me a couple of days ago."

"Touché."

Duke steps off the back porch, jerking his chin toward the landscaping he's kept occupied with. "So?"

"It looks amazing."

"Trick I picked up at an after-school job many moons ago."

I huff, crossing my arms as I do. "I wouldn't have the patience."

He's showered and changed since I saw him this morning, no doubt due to how sweaty he would have got doing all this in the unseasonal heat we had today. I push that mental image to the back of my brain, reminding myself he's a hothead, and hotheads come second to douche exes who don't deserve to be ogled anymore.

"Wasn't sure what you had planned for dinner, but I found some meat and whipped something up."

He needs to stop making me like him in this way. It's not fair. "You've done too much, honestly."

"Nonsense." He beckons toward the house. "Come inside and put your feet up. I'll get you a drink."

I narrow my gaze on him as he leads us in the back door, wondering what he's broken. "I'm not really thirsty. But thank you, though." Men are only this overly nice when they either need to apologise, or they want something. I'm not sure which thought disturbs me more.

"I spoke to Mum on the way home," I say as I pause to throw my bag in the bedroom.

"Yeah, she came over. She's real nice," he calls back from the living room. I walk in to find him kicked back on the sofa.

"She's nosey," I correct. Even more so than I bargained for when I sent her over. I asked her to check on *him,* not meddle with *me.*

Duke shrugs at my statement, lips twisted. "Not a bad thing. Means she cares, is all."

"Yeah ..." The word trails off as I reminisce about all the times her sticky beak *wasn't* helpful. "Did you complain to her about sleeping on the sofa?"

He snorts a laugh. "No. That was all your mum. She's concerned for my well-being." The smartarse winks at me.

I leave him with a huff, figuring I'll go see what he's murdering in the kitchen. "I told her not to worry about it since you sleep on the floor anyway."

Stone-cold silence surrounds me. I chance a look around the corner and find him staring at me, impassive. "You saw that, huh?"

"You weren't exactly trying to hide it." The aroma of beef fills my nostrils, pulling my focus back to the kitchen. He's found a small rolled roast I didn't even know I had, and has it in the oven surrounded by vegetables that look positively mouth-watering.

"I didn't know I had all this in the freezer," I call out,

choosing to ignore his discomfort.

"You didn't." Duke slips into what's fast becoming his usual spot: the barstool. "Your mum brought some 'real food' after she panicked that what you had in your cupboards couldn't 'sustain' a man like me." He bops his fingers in quotations as he recites my mother's words.

"Busy body."

"Like I said, she cares." His eyes follow my every move as I pull a wine glass from the cabinet and promptly fill it two-thirds with the half-drunk bottle that was in the fridge.

"I don't have any beer to offer you, sorry."

He lifts a hand, flashing me the palm. "All good. I don't drink alcohol anyway."

Unusual.

"So, Duke." I set my glass down, sliding it carefully to the side so as not to knock it over. "Why *do* you sleep on the floor?"

"Why is your second bedroom closed off?"

He doesn't miss a beat, this one. "Trade. You tell me, and then I'll tell you." My heart thunders at the offer, but hell, he'll be gone in a week, and then it'll just be me and my ghosts again.

His brow sets in a hard line as he leans forward, clasping his hands with his elbows rested on the counter. A heavy breath exits his nose as he seemingly weighs the proposition up. "You ready for this, Cammie?"

I pinch my bottom lip between my teeth and smirk. "I can take whatever you've got to throw at me."

"I wasn't talking about what *I've* got to say," he

counters. "Are you ready to pull back the covers and reveal what you've kept stored away?"

Fuck him. Fuck him and his unwavering sensibility. He's not afraid of recounting what it is that keeps him on edge; he's worried about *me*. And rightly so. My pulse doesn't throb painfully in my neck for no reason; my body temperature isn't elevated because I'm cool, calm, and collected. I'm freaking out, and I haven't voiced a goddamn thing yet.

"Just start before I change my mind," I snap, reaching for the wine.

He leans back with a long and laboured sigh as I down half the glass. "The short and sweet version is I was near crushed to death. A mortar took out the building I was in, and I came this close to losing my leg." He holds his fingers a hair's breadth apart. "The explosion killed two of my best friends, and the damage done to my lungs from the dust I inhaled in the aftermath means even the slightest chest infection has the potential to put me in hospital."

I was wrong: I was totally unprepared for that. Unprepared for how coldly and clinically he states the facts. How *detached* he is as he recounts the things that nearly killed him.

"Do you feel guilty?" Every story I've read that involved a returned serviceman always ends in the guilt they feel at being the one who's home, the one who made it back.

He nods. "A little, yeah. But mostly, frustrated."

"Why?"

"I never got a chance to fight back." His fingertips beat an urgent rhythm against the counter. "Our camp was attacked between patrols. After the unharmed dragged those of us still breathing out, we were immediately transferred to a safe medical facility. Some fuckhead blew half a dozen of us up, and I never even lifted a gun to retaliate."

So much concealed rage ... No wonder he fired up when I asked about his life in the army. He resents the fact he's not still there.

"You regret coming home." I round the counter to take the seat beside him.

Duke shrugs, his face blank as he stares vacantly at the counter. "I regret a lot of things."

"Holding on to that anger will only destroy you," I say quietly, almost as though I might spook him back into silence if I speak too loudly. "It's not healthy."

He turns his head, his shoulders hunched as he regards me. "What is it you're holding on to, Cam?"

I lift a finger, waggling it at him as I set my glass down again. "Nuh-uh, mister. You haven't actually answered my question yet."

"Why I sleep on the floor?"

"Right." I set my hands on my thighs and patiently wait him out.

Duke runs a finger along the patterns in the counter top, his lips twitching as he seems to think it over. "The short answer is nightmares. I don't know why, but when I'm on the floor, I feel more secure, as though there aren't as many points of vulnerability."

I rest an elbow on the counter, and prop my head in my hand. "What happens in your nightmares?" What makes him feel as though he's constantly open to attack?

"Stupid shit." He laughs bitterly.

"Duke …" I reach out with my free hand and cover one of his. Interestingly, he doesn't pull away. "It's not stupid if it bothers you that much."

"It is when the things don't even make sense." His thumb touches the side of my hand. "I dream of random crap, like my dead buddies sitting point on the slabs that pinned me down, shooting anyone who tries to get me out. I dream of faceless men smothering me until I can't breathe. An endless desert with a mirage of a cargo plane on the horizon that I can never seem to reach, no matter how long I spend dragging my broken body towards it."

"Guilt," I whisper. "They all signify what you told me—that you wish you could have done something to fight back, to have helped."

He swallows, jerking his shoulders as he slides his hand from under mine. "Doesn't change anything, knowing, does it?"

"What about help now you're back?" I ask, before downing the last of my wine and rising to pour another. "Mental health facilities? Surely you get some sort of assistance?"

"I do." He follows me to the fridge, pulling a bottle of water out after me. "Got myself a referral to a counsellor. Not sure if it'll help, but gotta try something, you know? First session is in two weeks."

"Sometimes an outside perspective helps. Like, they see things you can't because you're so used to viewing them the same way."

"Maybe."

I stand with my new wine in my hand as Duke

casually uncaps the bottle and chugs half the contents. He's really got to stop doing that around me, otherwise I'm not going to be held responsible for the inappropriate things it causes me to do, like, I don't know, lick his neck? Seriously ... the way that throat works ...

"You okay?" He smirks, clearly aware I'm embarrassed that he's caught me staring.

"Fine."

"So." He re-caps the bottle and puts it back in the fridge ... with the others.

Ugh. Keep it separate when it's been drunk from. Always separate. "So?"

"I told you mine ..."

Shit. So he has. My palms slicken with sweat as my heart threatens to crush my lungs in its escape from my chest.

Duke's smile fades, his eyes softening. "Hey, look. If it's too much—"

"No." I throw back the glass of wine, setting the empty vessel in the sink. "Let's do this."

Who better to face this with than a guy who doesn't know me, can't judge how I react based on who I was before? Somebody who's not as emotionally invested as the people I've slowly pushed away over the years: my mum, Dad, even Jared.

He still appears apprehensive, as though he's not entirely sure what he's set in motion as I walk past. Hell, *I'm* not sure what he's set in motion. I've stayed out of that room for close to two years now. I've avoided it at any costs, all while fiercely protecting its contents.

I stop before the door, my chest thick with regret as

I reach for the handle. My fingers make contact, yet before I can turn the old brass knob, a warm, calloused hand covers my own.

"I'm serious, Cammie. If you're not ready, don't do it."

"I'm ready," I whisper, wriggling my hand to indicate he should remove his.

Duke's warmth envelops the length of me, his chest brushing against my shoulder as shifts his weight. "Then why are you crying?"

Shit. Am I? *Shit, shit, shit.*

I wipe under my eye with the side of my finger, careful not to smudge my most likely ruined makeup. I already look crazy, getting so worked up over a room; there's no need to look as if I've completely lost the plot.

"Sorry. I ... shoot." I glance to the side, catching his presence in my periphery. "It's second nature some-times."

He takes a step back, nodding slowly. "Like I said, when *you're* ready."

No time like the present.

Before I have time to form a conscious protest in my mind, I twist and push, opening the room up to the rest of the house for the first time in years. Stale air hits me first, the smell something I could only describe as dusty. But what comes second on the undertones damn well breaks my heart all over again.

Strawberry: the tangy artificial kind that's synony-mous with all little girl's toy cosmetics and dolls.

I don't even try to hold back the tears, pretend they're not a part of who I am when I think of my baby.

The salty drops track across my cheeks, a badge of honour for the love I felt toward this tiny human. Proof I once succeeded in life.

"Taylah," I whisper. "Her name was Taylah."

Duke slips into the room behind me, his hand brushing mine as he ventures farther in to inspect her toy chest, her bed, and her lowboy still covered in her favourite plushies.

"How old was she?"

He doesn't say it, but the words hang in the untouched innocence of her haven: *when she died.*

"Four. She was six weeks shy of her fifth birthday." I let out a sad laugh, folding my arms across my chest as though it can save my heart from this pain. "We bought her school uniform already, had her enrolled. She was excited, ready to go and make new friends. You can see it if you open her wardrobe."

Duke stops by the window, using a single finger to edge the sheer curtains aside. He's probably working out how he didn't notice the contents of the room from the front of the house, how I manage to camouflage the fact that this was a family home once, that it *is* a family home.

"That the reason you split with your ex?"

"Yeah," I say on a sigh, daring to reach out and pinch her teddy's ear between my fingers. "Jared blames me. He couldn't look at me the same after."

As predicted, Duke's brow furrows, his eyes dark as he scowls. "That's shit, Cam. That's just shit. He was your husband, right?"

I nod.

"Then he should have fucking stuck by you. He

should have been there for you as much as I bet you were for him."

The tears come faster, harder, as I try to focus on this poor confused man before me. "I don't blame him, Duke. I don't fault him for leaving me."

"Why the fuck not?"

I smile, rolling my eyes as I sigh and try to gather myself a little better. "Because he's right." My chin crumples as I smile through the pain, just as I always do. "It *was* my fault. If it weren't for me, she wouldn't have died. I killed her."

SIXTEEN

DUKE

THE FUCK SHE TALKING ABOUT? SHE KILLED HER daughter? What the hell is this, *The Twilight Zone*? Because this sleepy town full of friendly people seriously hides one fucked up secret.

"Come again?" I step a little closer, as though *that's* going to help me understand what she just said.

"It was my fault, Duke." She storms from the room, leaving me to chase after her to hear what she says next. "My negligence meant she died." Cammie swipes a tissue from the box in the bathroom drawer, wiping her eyes. "If I'd paid more attention, thought about it, I could have prevented the whole damn thing from happening." She talks to me, although it's herself she stares at angrily in the mirror as she wipes away her smudged makeup.

"Tell me what happened." I take a seat on the side of the tub. "Explain it to me so I can make up my own mind if you're to blame, because, Cam, I don't think you could be."

She sighs, her hands on the vanity as she hangs her head between her shoulders. "How long has the roast got to go?"

Fucking woman. "Don't ignore the question."

"I'm not," she snaps before sighing and repeating the words a lot softer. "I'm not. I'm just hungry, and quite frankly, this whole thing is upsetting enough; you don't want to add 'Hangry Cammie' to the mix."

Damn woman makes me chuckle, as much as I'd rather not. "Fair enough. Let's go check."

She fluffs around, fixing her eyeliner or some shit while I head back to the kitchen and check the rolled beef. Sure enough, the thing's ready to go—too much longer and it would have been tough as an old gumboot.

"So?" Cammie asks as she finally re-joins me.

"You were right to ask. It's ready."

She gives me a smug rise of one eyebrow, and then moves across to the far side of the living room as I pull the stainless-steel tray from the oven and set it down on top of the sink. After what feels like an hour of searching in what I thought would be the obvious places, I give up trying to locate a carving fork and use two knives: one stabbed through the roll to keep it in place, and one to cut it.

All the while, Cammie ferrets around in the sideboard cabinets, pulling things out in her mad search for something. I keep a cursory eye on her as I plate the meat and vegetables, transferring the tray to the stovetop to make gravy from the juices.

The look on her face when I set the plates on the table makes every ounce of the effort worth it.

"I should keep you on," she says with a smile, despite the fact her eyes are puffy and red, her pinked cheeks giving away how she really feels. "I thought you said you couldn't cook?"

"Cook? No. Can't add anything together without it tasting nothing like it should. But make a mean as roast? Easy."

"Says you."

I chuckle as I pull out her seat.

Cammie takes her place at the table graciously, reaching up to set some papers on the surface beside her place setting. I take my seat opposite her, and indicate for her to start.

"I don't usually say grace or anything," she says as she slices into the meat. *Straight for the best parts.* "So I hope you're not offended."

"Neither." I take a mouthful of roast potato drenched in gravy and groan. I haven't had a roast in what feels like forever. "Damn that's good, if I do say so myself."

Cammie nods in agreement, her eyes closed. "Mm-hmm."

I wait until she's looking at me again and jerk my chin at the papers. "What are they?"

She pops a carrot in her mouth and then sets her knife down to unfold the top sheet. With her palm flat over the contents, she slides it across the table to me, gesturing for me to read it as she picks up her knife and continues to eat.

I take a bite of the meat and chew it slowly as I look over the newspaper article. It's short—probably a bare mention halfway through their local rag, but it's to the point, that's for sure. The headline reads: **LOCAL WOMAN UNDER INVESTIGATION AFTER TRAGIC ACCIDENT.**

"Jared saved it for me," she explains between

mouthfuls. "At the start, I couldn't face anything that would remind me of it, so I'd bin the paper when it was delivered before I even unrolled it from the plastic. He fished it out and clipped that for when I was better."

I run my eye over the column as she speaks.

"He said he saved it at first because he thought it might make me see that I did everything I could." She pauses, waiting for me to finish.

The article outlines in brief detail the events that led to her daughter, Taylah's, death. An innocent enough day, by the looks of things, that ended in tragedy when her daughter ran down the driveway to the open road and was struck by a car. The woman under investigation wasn't Cammie, as I'd first assumed; it was the driver of the car that hit her little girl.

"But then this one came out." She slides the next sheet of newsprint across to me. The article's a fair sight longer. "He never looked at or spoke to me the same after that." Her eyes fixate on the printed letters, her thoughts clearly somewhere else. Or maybe they're here, trapped in a nightmare that came to life a long time ago.

MOTHER ACCUSED OF NEGLECT AFTER TODDLER'S DEATH

"Shit, Cam." I pull the article closer, setting my fork down on the side of my plate.

She continues with her meal in silence as I read the words that damn her involvement beyond any shadow of a doubt.

"It was an accident," she whispers as I reach the end. "It's not as though I set it all up, planned it, or did any of it knowing what would happen. How was I to know?"

"You say that, and yet you still blame yourself?"

Cammie pushes her plate aside, setting both elbows on the table so she can cover her face with her hands. "Because I should have been more careful, Duke. I should have thought about it when I took the cold and flu medicine."

My appetite lost, I lean back in my seat and pick the article up to read it again. According to the report, Cammie was on a nightly dose of prescribed medication for insomnia at the time. After taking additional drugs for a head cold during the day, the ingredients reacted and left her drowsy and unable to be roused when she fell asleep. Her daughter—*their* daughter—opened the front door and made her way to the road where the accident with the car occurred. The driver was cleared of the charges of careless driving causing death considering the open road speed limit, and the hedge that obscured the driveway meant she had no chance of reacting in time to avoid the collision.

"Cammie."

"What?" she moans, still hiding behind her hands.

"Look at me."

A moment passes where I wonder if she's going to up and walk out, yet she finally drops her hands with a sigh revealing bloodshot eyes.

"Are you listening?"

She nods.

I hold her gaze, make sure I don't blink, and say, "It. Wasn't. Your. Fault."

Her nostrils flare, those perfectly sculpted brows twitching as she slowly but surely begins to shake her head. "You don't get it, do you?"

"I think I do." My knife and fork hit the plate with

more force than I intended as I slice into the nearly cold roast. "You were a mother trying to feel well enough to care for the child she loved above anything else. Also, a mother who needed sleep to function. Nothing unusual, Cam. Nothing to feel bad about."

Her jaw hangs as she stares at me finishing my meal. A few choked sounds come out, but other than that, I've got her.

This time she walks out. Her chair scrapes across the floor as she rises with a huff, abandoning her unfinished dinner to stride from the room. Using the side of my finger, I wipe up the last of the gravy, not wasting an ounce of this meal while I give her a moment. Her frustrated howls echo down the hallway as I stand, and then clear the table, carrying both plates to the kitchen to begin the clean-up.

I don't even get as far as retrieving the dishwashing tools from the pantry before a telltale crash has me heading through to the hallway. Glass litters the timber floor, the shards catching the spill of light from the living room. I look to the left in time to catch Cammie as she reaches up and yanks another picture off its hook, lifting the treasured memory over her head before throwing it to the floor with a roar.

"Hey!"

The third and final picture resists, its wire caught up on the brass hook. Taking care not to get broken glass in my foot, I step over the carnage and take her forearms in my hands. "Stop, Cam."

"Let go of me!" She snarls, a cornered dog looking for a way out.

"No." My hands tighten, her skin bunching in my

hold. Fuck, I'm probably bruising the woman, but like hell I'm walking away from this when I'm partially responsible for starting it.

Fuck my curiosity. Fuck her mother, too, for validating the idea in my head. Why the hell would she want me to crack this case of shit open if this is the reaction it gets? Surely she knows how much talking about it upsets Cammie? What parent would willingly inflict pain on their child like this?

One who wants change.

I know that process all too well, don't I?

"Just let me do this," Cammie moans as she wilts in my hold, her knees hitting the floor. "I need to do this."

"No, you don't." I loop one arm under hers, hefting her to her feet. "All you're going to do is regret this in the morning." She doesn't fight me when I guide her away from the mess and toward her bedroom. "I get you've got to work through it, but destroying the things you have left isn't the answer."

Her breath hiccups as I set her down on the edge of her bed. The room is exactly as I guessed: white and grey. A calming space for a woman who's nothing but frenetic chaos on the inside.

"Can I trust you to get into your pyjamas if I leave you alone?"

She nods, already removing the tie from her hair.

"Good. Now where's your dustpan? In the fridge?"

She chuckles, exactly as I'd hoped.

"No, you muppet. It's in the hall cupboard."

Of course. "Get changed, Cam. I'll be back in ten."

She rolls onto her back as I step out and pull the door shut behind me. Soft sniffles filter through the wall as I kneel and rescue the prints from the mess on her floor. My chest tightens as I take stock of the images properly for the first time. I'd looked before, but never *looked* at what the images contained.

A woman surrounded by love.

A mother whose world was complete.

A perfect stranger's life before it was torn away in the blink of an eye.

Just like mine.

SEVENTEEN

First Corporal Piata looked at the envelope in his hand, at the torn edge that signified the contents had been checked over and approved to go through the internal mail to reach the base in the middle of Buttfuck, Nowhere.

He hated dust. Hated it when he was home and renovating the old state house that he'd managed to buy with his wife before he re-deployed six months ago. Hated it even more now that the fucking stuff was ingrained in every pore of his body. It wasn't even sand, like you got on the beaches at home; they were the fine granules that stuck to your nose hairs when you were sandblasting an old car. The gritty, unforgiving kind.

He pulled the scarf that permanently sat around his neck over his mouth and nose, and pushed the exit door to cross over to the mess hall. His unit had rolled in a little under an hour ago, most of the men heading straight to wash away as much of the road grime as they could before filling their guts with the basic fare the kitchen served night after night.

The evening was cool, nothing unusual for the

desert. But something else lurked in the lazy breeze that made dust devils in the yard. Something unsettling.

His gaze dropped to the letter again as apprehension took hold of his throat. He hated being the bearer of bad news, had resented it since he was the one to let his mum know that Uncle Benny had passed away at the local RSA after a heart attack. Grief was an unforgiving bride, sweeping in and taking you for all you had.

And the guy who had an imminent wedding date with the bitch? Yeah, he didn't deserve this. It was always the good ones who seemed to lump all the bad luck.

"Just in time, you fat bastard," his buddy called out as Piata stepped into the hall and shook his scarf off.

"Yeah, bro. Another five minutes and I bet you would have eaten all the vanilla pudding, hey?"

Fuck, he hated this. Duke was his best mate, his buddy who kept the miserable assholes laughing when the reality of life in the desert got them down. He was so happy, so unaware that in less than sixty seconds his whole world would change.

"I, uh, I picked this up for you, man." Piata handed the envelope over; staying close for the fallout he knew would come.

Shit, Duke could take all the hate and rage out on him if he so wished, and he'd stand there and take it, because fuck it, wasn't that what best mates were for?

"What is it?" his buddy asked, lifting the torn edge. "You read it, you dirty dog?"

"Nah, man, but I was warned what's in it."

All traces of humour slid from Duke's face, his arse hitting the table behind him as he stared at Piata.

"What, bro?"

"Read it." Piata jerked his chin at the envelope, wishing he hadn't stopped by the admin building. Maybe then he wouldn't have felt obligated to take the job. Maybe then somebody else would have. But isn't bad news the kind of thing you'd rather get from a friend?

Duke slid his finger between the edges of the envelope, pulling out the single sheet of paper from inside. He unfolded it, smoothing the creases as he began to read.

Fuck—why didn't somebody phone this one in? Piata understood how things worked, knew that calls on the Sat-phone were few and far between. Especially when they couldn't be sure who was listening in while they were stationed in the middle of nowhere. But shit, this kind of news by letter? What fucking year was it? 1954?

"Bro, tell me this is some sick joke." Unshed tears rimmed Duke's eyes as he held the sheet of paper between them. "You fuckers getting in early for my birthday?"

Piata said nothing, just shook his head at his best mate.

"Tell me!" Duke roared, throwing the letter down. "Say it, you fucking cunt! 'This is a joke, Duke.' Say it!"

He wished he could. He wished more than anything the words "drunk driver" and "Duke's wife" had never been said to him in the same sentence, but they had, and all he could do now was stay with his best friend while he rode out the storm.

"It's real, bro." Piata reached out, placing a hand on

his mate's shoulder and squeezing hard. "I'm so fucking sorry. I know you loved her."

Duke's eyes rolled back as he stared at the ceiling, trying to compose himself. "Them, man. Them. She was pregnant."

Fuck.

EIGHTEEN

CAMMIE

DUKE KNOCKS ON THE DOOR AS I SETTLE IN BED with my back against the headboard. "You decent?"

"Yeah. Come in."

He opens the door cautiously, his gaze averted anyway. "I brought you something that might help with the eyes." He circles the index finger on his free hand at my face.

I watch with keen interest as he sets a coffee mug wrapped in a tea towel down on the nightstand. Four spoon handles protrude from the ice-chilled water that fills the mug.

"What do I do with it?"

He grins, tipping his head slightly. "You've never done this before?"

"Would I ask if I had?"

He huffs out his nose, picking out two ice-cold teaspoons. "Lean your head back and shut your eyes."

I do as I'm told, grumbling, "This sounds like the start of a bad prank."

Arctic metal encases my eyelids. "Fuck me, Duke! You could have warned me." My hands shoot up in front of me, colliding with one very warm, very hard body.

"Trust me, it works to reduce the puffiness. My mum used to do it all the time when we were kids."

"All the time?" I can barely stand doing it once. "Did she enjoy it that much?" I joke.

"No," he states in such a tone that I can imagine his blank face as he does. "Dad enjoyed making her cry that often, though."

Damn … Didn't see that coming. "I'm sorry, I didn't—"

"It's fine." His weight shifts onto the edge of the bed. "Take these off me, yeah?"

I reach up, a little more cautious this time, and fumble around until I have the handles in my grasp. Duke's hands slide out from under mine, yet his weight stays on my bed. *Interesting.*

"When they warm up, swap them for the other ones, and then repeat until the water isn't cold enough to cool them down anymore."

"And this will get rid of my red eyes?"

"Mm-hmm. Stops the swelling so you don't wake up tomorrow looking like you're allergic to bees."

"Gee, thanks," I deadpan.

He sits silently for a while, so quiet that I edge one of my legs across until it bumps into what I assume is his butt.

"I'm still here," he murmurs.

Three little words, and he seals the hole in my heart. I barely know this guy from Adam, and yet he's managed to make more progress towards helping me get closure than my family has in the past three years.

The spoons warm, and I peel them off to change

them over, blinking as the light hits my adjusted retinas. Duke reaches out and takes the spoons from me, exchanging them for the cold ones.

"You can hit the hay, if you like," I say. "I'll be okay now."

He seems as though he's about to take the subtle hint, yet instead he places his hands over mine and gently guides the spoons to my eyes. "Ten more minutes to be sure can't hurt."

Why the hell couldn't Jared have been this awesome? Maybe there's truth to the saying that anything worth having is also worth waiting for? Because I feel as though I've waited a lifetime for a man like Duke.

"You know, I was thinking while I got changed that we could rearrange the living room," I say.

"Why?" His weight shifts a little farther onto the mattress, his leg pressed against mine.

"I thought if I shifted the sofa by the window around to face the other one, and then shunted them both to the wall, it would make a little cave for you to sleep in. A safe space."

He doesn't say a thing.

My heart thunders in my ears, my other senses heightened while my sight is trapped in the dark. Panic engulfs me when I wonder if I made him mad. But then again, he hasn't left. His leg still presses on mine, his weight still causing the mattress to dip and me to lean toward him.

I swallow, the spoons warm, and yet the fear of what I'll find if I take them away forces me to keep them in place. My tongue sweeps across my lips, words failing me as I fight for what to say to accept I probably overstepped the mark making his problem mine like that.

Turns out I don't need to say a thing at all.

The bed rolls as he moves. I prepare for him to leave, for the click of the door as he goes.

I don't prepare for warm lips to press against my own. I sure as hell don't prepare for the way his gentle caress makes my heart skip a beat, or how I lean forward to keep the connection a little longer as he pulls away.

Wow. Totally didn't predict that.

The spoons hit the bed as I blink rapidly, willing my eyes to stop their ridiculous burn at the sudden intrusion of light.

Duke sits still as a statue, watching me as I re-join the room.

"Are you going to say something?" I whisper.

"I don't know what to say." His brow furrows, his eyes almost alarmed.

"Shit, Duke. You sure know how to make a girl feel awkward."

I look away as he falters for words, and focus on the inane task of swapping the spoons over. If he's not sure how he feels about what he just did, then why *did* he? I didn't ask him to kiss me. I don't think I did anything to instigate that kind of situation. What the hell is his deal?

"Cam," he says, strong and sure.

"What, Duke?" I spin my heated gaze to him, maddened that he's gone and made what was already a tense night worse.

"You didn't stop me." He frowns. "You should have stopped me."

"I should have stopped you?" I roll my eyes, slapping the cold spoons over them immediately after. "Is that all you're thinking right now?" I snap, aware I probably look like a lunatic going off my chain at him with spoons over my eyes. "You think it was up to *me* to stop you?" I huff, growing madder by the second. "Newsflash, buddy. It's the twenty-first century. Men should be able to control themselves without blaming their lust on the girl involved."

He ignores my rambling, and continues with his lame protest. "Why didn't you push me off?"

Heat rushes through my body, settling low in my abdomen at the thought of why. "Because"—I swallow— "I liked it."

He doesn't say anything, simply hums as though the idea interests him.

"Let me guess," I say. "That makes me a hussy, allowing some stranger to come on to me in my *own* bedroom." I laugh, feeling the need to steer this somewhere a little more light-hearted. "Jeez, Duke. If you wanted a comfier place to sleep, you could have just said you changed your mind about swapping for the bed."

He doesn't laugh with me, not even a snort. *Think I'll stay behind these spoons forever.*

"You talk too much. You know that?"

Well aware, buddy.

"You keep shit in weird places," he continues, "and you eat rat-shit kids food that has no real nutritional value for you."

"Anything else?" I drone.

"You hold on to ghosts that keep you isolated from everyone who loves you, and you drive like a fucking maniac."

I sigh, resting my head against the headboard. "You know, this isn't doing anything to help make me feel better about myself."

"I know," he says as though exasperated by the train of thought tumbling from his lips. "I'm not trying to be an arsehole, Cam."

I drop the spoons, yet keep my eyes shut for one more blissful minute. "Then what *are* you trying to do, Duke?"

He sighs, getting off the bed. I set the spoons aside and open my eyes. He stands with his back to me, as though he's ready to walk out but for some unknown reason, he can't find it in himself to physically do so. His head drops, and he looks to the floor as he admits the reason for this detailing of my faults. "You drive me crazy with your annoying habits, Cam, and yet ..."

Yet? I scoot up in the bed, holding on for his next words.

"And yet that piece-of-shit car breaking down was the best thing that's happened to me in a hell of a long time."

I fold the covers back and move to the edge of the bed, hanging my legs over the side as an amused smile curls my lips up on one side. "Why, Duke. Would that be a compliment you just gave me?"

His laugh is low and throaty, supressed. "I guess."

What is it about this man that he can't let himself loosen up? I get that he's angry about what happened to him, but damn, live a little, laugh.

He drops a frustrated sigh as he runs a hand through his hair. "I put those pictures on top of your sideboard. Figured you could reframe them when you felt the time was right." He takes a step toward the door and hesitates, looking back at me over his shoulder. "Get some sleep, okay?"

"Sure. Thank you for the spoons." I give him a soft smile and let him go, more for his own relief than mine.

I could have kept him close for longer, picked his brain and possibly, maybe, got him to kiss me again. But I'm not blind; he needs space to think things through. He needs to work out exactly how he feels about what just went down.

As do I.

Sleep. Yeah, I won't be doing much of that. Taylah's death cemented two things for me: one, endless sleepless nights where, if I'm lucky, I snatch a few rough hours, and two, that I will never ever take medication to aid my insomnia again.

After all, why should I sleep when my baby is doing enough for the both of us?

NINETEEN

DUKE

All she had to say was one little thing about a damn sofa and I lost focus of why this woman can only ever be a passing phase in my life. We're so different, yet she selflessly offered to do something that makes *me* feel better, and I'm left with a burning gratitude for how effortlessly kind she is.

She gives her love without expectation of reward, offering only the best part of her. Even when that douchebag ex came over to bully her into picking an estate agent, she never faltered. She could have sliced that sharp tongue of hers across his wounds and cut him down, thrown the fact that the arsehole left her when she needed him most in his face, but she didn't.

Because that's not Cam.

When you're blessed with the ability to feel love and empathy to such a level, you're also cursed to wear the scars such connection brings. No wonder the woman guards her pain so fiercely. She's not just unable to move on for fear of losing the last connection she has to her daughter—she's afraid of spreading her pain to the people she loves.

She's afraid of influencing others' lives in a negative way.

One more reason why we're so different. All I do is layer my anger and resentment over those around me, unsatisfied until they understand why I can never let go of the misery and hate I carry at how that one event ruined so many lives.

With my arse to the timber, I scoot my back into the junction of the sofa and the wall and do my ritual sweep of the room. How long will I be like this? Living in fear despite the fact I'm halfway around the world from where the real threat of attack resides?

This isn't how to live. It's not how a man behaves. Shit, if my father could see me now he'd hang his head in shame. I might have lost respect for the arsehole when he cut my mother down and left to be with his mistress, but he still stamped the basic macho beliefs in me that no matter how hard I try, I can't shake.

Men don't cry.

Men don't whine about their troubles to whoever will listen.

Real men stick their proverbial middle fingers up to the world that treads on them, and battle on.

I *should* be battling on, but here I am, sitting in a stranger's house, thinking about what a waste my life is. My future was in army greens. My destiny was to either die young or retire when my ravaged and beaten body couldn't take another tour. I had purpose, an outlet for my anger. I had respect.

I had the love of a good woman to return to. A new family.

Now ... *nothing.* I'm nothing, nobody. And worst of

all, I contribute nothing to this world. I suck oxygen, I eat produce, but what do I give back?

So many bad things are happening right now, so many fights for survival taking place this very second, and where am I? Huddled under a blanket looking for the fucking bogeyman.

Goddamn fucking disgrace.

I reach across and pick up my phone—torch on as always. The light illuminates my lap as I tap out a message to Cody.

How's that cash coming along?

Knowing the dork, he's probably still awake playing Xbox. Sure enough, three dots dance on my screen.

Sorry, bro. Not this week.

For fuck's sake. I tap out half a dozen replies, deleting each before I send them. There's no point getting mad at him, because just like our old man, he doesn't give a shit if he puts you out. It's all for him, and all about him.

A week or hopefully less, and I'll be out of here and on my way to doing something for me. If I only I knew what the fuck that was.

◆ ◆ ◆

"Duke."

Nudge. Nudge.

"Duke."

Fuck me, I've been asleep? Feels as though I only just drifted off. "What time is it?"

"Eight. I have to leave for work, but I've left you some breakfast in the oven."

Cammie stands over me, gorgeous as always in a pair of black leggings, an over-sized white shirt, and a cropped cardigan. The boots on her feet are almost as big as she is, covered in studs and buckles. I've never paid much mind to women's fashion before, but this girl certainly knows how to dress to bring out her best assets: legs that go on for days, and a trim waist that's offset by her rounded arse and full tits. She's every man's perfect hourglass.

"In the oven?" I rub my hands over my face with a yawn.

"Yeah, to keep it warm."

Cooked breakfast. She's turning more and more into wife material. "Thanks, Cam."

"I've left you something else as well." The keys in her hand rattle as she darts across to the table, returning a short time later with a notebook. "I was thinking about how you said you had counselling starting soon, and I know when I had some sessions after Taylah, that I'd get there and my mind would go blank." She smiles, despite looking at the book in her hands with sad eyes. "The therapist would ask me all these questions, and I'd sit there like a mute. So, I thought maybe if you wrote down your nightmares, your thoughts even, then you'd have material to talk about." She thrusts the notebook at me, a pen tucked into its spine.

I take the offered gift, feeling incredibly rude that I'm still seated on the floor ... but morning wood. What else can I do, but wait it out?

"Thanks." I set the book aside, not too sure how writing and I mix.

She frowns a little, cocking her head to the side. "It was just an idea. But I've got to go, so I'll see you tonight, yeah?"

"Sure."

She paces from one foot to the other and lets out a cute little huff. "Damn it."

I can't help but chuckle as she squats down and then leans forward, bracing her weight on her hands as she stretches toward me. Her crisp eyes hold mine, seemingly brighter given the dark liner she's ringed them with.

"Come on, Duke. Don't leave me hanging."

I know what she wants, and yeah, I'm stoked that she's got the balls to be so forward about it. But that doesn't mean I'm not arsehole enough to play with her a little just so I can hear her *say* it. "Hanging how? What's the matter?" I feign confusion at why she's crouched down, leant over my legs like this.

"Duke ..."

"You've got something in your eye?" I squint a little as I check out each one.

"Don't be an arse." Her arms start to shake as she holds her position.

"Tell me what you want, Cam." I steady my breathing, waiting on those words from her delicate lips: *for you to kiss me.*

"I want proof that it wasn't a mistake," she says instead.

Oh, I can do that. Kissing her last night might have

taken me by surprise, but it was no mistake. How can it be when I reacted on raw instinct alone?

I reach out and place my hands on her hips, pulling her forward so she's forced to drop to her knees. Cammie slides in closer as I urge her forward, her knees pressed tight against my thigh. She's poised, ready for my next move, when a relatively important thought pops into my head. "Do I have morning breath?"

"What?" she says with a laugh, her eyes crinkling adorably at the corners.

"I mean, I'd hate for this epic moment to be ruined by a bad experience with halitosis. Maybe I should go brush my teeth real quick."

She sighs out her nose, holding a single finger up. I watch as she dives into her bag and pulls out a tin of breath mints. A small blue tab drops into her hand, and pinching it between forefinger and thumb, she jerks her chin toward me. "Open up."

The mint burns on the tip of my tongue as she drops it on, dissolving quickly as I crunch it between my teeth and shift the powder all around my mouth. I huff into my cupped hand, satisfied with the result.

"Okay now?" she queries.

"Think so." Her breath hitches as I trail a fingertip under her jaw. "Where were we then?"

"You were about to convince me that you didn't kiss me by accident, that you don't regret it, and that the thought of your lips on mine has plagued you as much as the thought of mine on yours has driven me crazy this morning."

"Come here." I tuck my index finger under her jaw,

pressing into the soft flesh to coax her forward.

Her lids droop, her pupils flaring into deep black pools as she looks down to focus on my mouth. The sight of her so focused on our kiss does nothing to make the stiffy in my boxers disappear. If anything, the velvety feel of her painted lips as she teases them against mine only thickens my cock until I'm twice as hard as I was when I woke up.

Inhibitions and doubts aside, I kiss this girl as if it's the first time we've met, as though neither of us are chained to the ghosts of our pasts, and as though somewhere, somehow, in an alternate reality, chalk and cheese like Cam and I could actually get along enough to have a future together.

She shifts the knee closest to me between my legs, settling herself on my thigh. I groan as the warmth at the apex of her thighs heats my leg, her pussy pressed flush against my quad. *Grind it, baby.* The thought settles in my mind as she pinches my bottom lip between hers, soft, slow, sensual.

Grind those hips, girl.

"Duke ..."

"Yeah?" *Don't get off.*

"We're stopping it here."

I groan. "Why?"

She smiles, those eyes bright as she does indeed climb off and straighten her clothes. "I'm convinced."

Damn it's good to see those eyes bright again. "Good."

Cammie collects her bag and keys, tossing the set in her hand as she seems to think over what to say next. She chooses not to speak, which is fine by me, because to be honest, I don't know what to say either.

I met this woman four days ago. It hasn't even been a week, and yet, I'm struck by how easy it is to connect with her. Especially since we both faced our fears and shared with each other the innermost parts of who we are.

Who we were.

Maybe who we can be.

Only time will tell.

TWENTY

I roll my eyes at Mum's statement. She wouldn't come out and actually say it, but I know what she hints at—she's usually lucky if I call her twice in a week. I'm so stubbornly independent.

"Well, because I'm sure your visit yesterday had a little something to do with it, I thought I'd share a milestone with you."

"You learned how to shop for real food?" She laughs at her own joke.

"No, Mum." I take deep breath, twisting my grip on the steering wheel. "I opened Taylah's door."

She falls so quiet, I have to check the dashboard display to make sure I haven't dropped the call. "Mum?"

"How did you go?" she asks softly. "Are you okay today?"

Truthfully? No, I'm not. I spent the majority of the day at work stumbling my way through my tasks with the blind focus of a zombie. My thoughts were trapped amongst the images of Taylah the day she died at her kiddie table, eating her lunch. The last positive memory

I have of her, considering what we did in the following hour was never more than a blur. The next clear memory I can dredge up is the flash of blue and red as I opened my eyes to an officer shaking me awake.

They thought I had overdosed. I wish I had.

"She's been on my mind a lot, but I think I'm okay with that."

"Duke?" she says. "What did he do?"

"Talked me off a ledge." A smile creeps onto my lips as I think back to this morning. "He was great about it all, really."

"That's good, honey. I'm honestly so glad to hear it."

"You know," I say with slight jest to my tone, "it's a bit low to enlist the help of a stranger like that."

"He's a nice boy," she protests. "And it worked, didn't it?"

"I guess."

She lets the silence hang a while as I drive, my thoughts a jumbled mess. Taylah, Jared, the house sale, and now Duke. So many things demanding attention at once.

"Is there something else?" Mum asks carefully.

"Jared wants me to sell the house."

Her sharp intake of air is deafening in the confines of my car. "Why? He agreed to let you stay there as long as you covered the mortgage on your own. What does he want with it now? I knew we should have forced him to transfer his name off the documents."

"We couldn't, remember? To do that I would have had to draw down again, and I didn't have the lending power on my own to do that."

"Yes, I do remember now." She sighs. "Damn it, Cam.

What are you going to do? I hope you're going to fight his sorry arse."

"I tried, but he doesn't want to hear about it."

"How long has this been going on?" Mum asks.

"A couple of weeks."

"And you're only telling me now? Cam ..."

I sigh, fingers flexing on the wheel. "I thought I might be able to talk him out of it, make him see reason and the whole thing would blow over. But I can't. The sale is going ahead."

She hesitates before saying quietly, "Maybe it's for the best. Everything happens for a reason, sweetheart."

"I know. I'm just not ready yet, you know?" I take a deep breath and hold strong before I let myself slip into the past once more. "I told him to list the house with an agent who's related to Kell."

"Cammie," Mum drones. "What would you do that for? She'll be biased."

"Exactly. He wouldn't let her get away with a cheaper price in the name of a quick sale, so if I have to sell, I may as well make the most profit I can out of it." Perhaps, given inflation over the past five years, I'll walk away with enough to put a healthy deposit on another old villa, this time on a smaller property, so I can follow through with my B&B idea. *Got to look for that silver lining.*

"What's the asking price?"

"Why, Mum?"

"What's the asking price?" she repeats more matter-of-fact.

I sigh, shifting gears to turn into the driveway. "The last rateable valuation put the house and land at a bit over four hundred thousand."

"I'll talk to your father," she says before promptly hanging up.

"Mum!"

It's no use. She's left me with that statement knowing I'd give her heaps about the crazy plan she's no doubt cooking. She can't afford to buy it, let alone be a guarantor for me. But Dad … Dad has the lending power, and she knows I'd never ask him for a huge helping hand like that. *Damn it all.*

I park the car and then head into the house to find Duke, find out what he's been up to today. Hearing him talk about anything at all sounds like heaven. He could recite the things he ate in chronological order and I'd be grateful for the distraction.

The place is quiet as I set my bag down on the side table in the entrance, save for the sound of running water.

Not going there, Cammie. Totally not thinking about my stranded traveller in the shower … naked … wet.

"I'm home!" I call out, as much to take my mind off the visuals I'm conjuring up as to let Duke know.

"In the shower!"

Lord, baby Jesus …

Fanning myself with one hand I make my way through to the living room and come to a grinding halt. The sofas have been rearranged exactly how I suggested, but on top of that, he's pulled some of my framed pictures of Taylah and me out of the sideboard and arranged them on the lamp table.

My arse hits the seat cushion as I collapse and reach for the foremost photo. I forgot about this one, how it used to be my favourite. She's so pretty, all decked out in her overalls and gumboots as she helps Jared clean the back porch with the water blaster. The photo's just of her though; I wouldn't know Jared were there if the day wasn't set in my memories.

Twenty-five degrees and not a cloud in the sky. We'd planned to visit his parents, but because it was the first fine Saturday we'd had in weeks, we took the opportunity to do odd jobs around the house instead. The two of them—father and daughter—finished off the last of the work for the day, late afternoon, while I ducked inside to prepare dinner. I'd happened to step out to check on Taylah, make sure she wasn't getting in Jared's way, but I couldn't pass up the opportunity to take a snap.

Thank God I did. Where would I be now if I'd just smiled and enjoyed the moment at the time, not saving it for later?

For forever?

"Hey." Duke's quiet greeting startles me out of my state of reminiscing.

"Hey."

He takes a seat opposite me, watching me carefully, as though searching for clues as to how I really feel about this. "You can put them back if you like."

"No, it's good," I tell him, resolute in my answer. "If you hadn't pulled the pictures out, I don't know if I ever would have."

He makes a small humming noise as he leans back in the seat, his hair still damp, and his skin holding a slight flush from the heat of the shower.

"This one," I say, handing him the picture of Taylah.

"It's my favourite. She was helping her dad clean the porch out there." I point toward the back of the house.

"Cute." He smiles, but I can tell it's that forced kind of compliment from a person who can see a child's appeal to others, yet doesn't actually *like* children.

Duke passes the picture back, pointing to the one behind as I set it back on the table. "I like that one of you both. It's natural, more special."

"Yeah." *Another treasured memory.* "My mum took that at Dad's birthday party."

"Your parents still together?"

"No. But they're friends."

"Hmm." He twists his lips to the side. "Must be nice."

He sounds bitter. "Makes things less confrontational, definitely." I give him a moment to say something, yet he stays silent, staring at the pictures on the table. "Was it hard for you, when your father left? I mean, you said he wasn't all that nice."

"So you're wondering if I was relieved?"

When you put it like that ... "Yeah."

Duke's chest rises as he takes a deep breath and spreads his arms across the back of the sofa. "I didn't miss him, but I also wasn't happy that he'd left, if that makes sense."

"I think I understand."

The silence between our stunted dialogue echoes louder with each pause we take. Maybe two tough nights in a row, when it comes to conversation, isn't such a flash idea.

"Any clue what we should make for dinner tonight?" I ask, putting as much cheer into my words as I can.

"You pick." His eyes find mine, the expression there

not one I can read. Is he irritated that I asked about his dad? Is he annoyed to still be here? Is he pissed that I've essentially avoided talking about what happened this morning and placed us squarely back in the "friends" box?

"Well, tomorrow will be a meal on the run because I've got a fundraising event to be at straight after work, so I guess I should pick something healthy tonight to make sure I'm not eating too much junk. Not that I was thinking of doughnuts and candy or anything insane like that, but you know what I mean."

Duke smiles.

"What?" I ask. Why is talking about dinner so amusing? "You asked me what I wanted us to have for dinner, and I was thinking out loud instead of sitting here looking rude, as though I was ignoring you."

"Nothing, Cam."

"Didn't look like nothing. I mean, you wouldn't just smirk at me like that if it was. You must have thought about something amusing to start smiling like an idiot."

He keeps going, his lips spreading into a wicked grin.

"Tell me," I cry, nudging his knee with my foot. "Do I have something on my face? Is my hair all blown into a bird's nest?" I feign shock. "I know—there's someone behind me, isn't there."

He chuckles, pushing off the seat to stand. "Nah, babe." His fingertips brush my knee as he passes by on his way to the kitchen. "It's nice seeing you back to normal, is all."

"Normal?" I ask, following him. "What do you mean by 'normal'?"

He takes a bottle of water from the fridge and holds

it between his hands. "I mean, you're chatty, smiling. You've got that, that"—he winds a hand at my face—"sparkle about you."

"Sparkle." I snort. "I'm not a unicorn, Duke. Missing my fairy wings as well, if that was your preference."

"Glow, then. You've got a glow. Although that's the kind of thing I'd say to a pregnant woman, and unless you've yet to share something with me, I'm sure that's not you."

"Well ..." I bite my lip and frown.

The panic that washes through him head to toe is nothing short of hilarious. "Cam, you better not be fucking with me."

"Why?" I ask feigning naïve innocence.

He sets the unopened bottle down on the counter, his eyes hooded as he sizes me up. "Because ..." He takes a step toward me. "One: it makes me wonder who the fuck the douche is that would knock a woman up and then walk. And two: if you were kidding—which I think you are—you're gonna pay for making a fool out of me." He approaches, doing a fine job of making himself appear bigger and more menacing as he closes in with a cheeky smile. "Who's the guy, Cam?"

"No guy." Nerves have me giggling like a damn schoolgirl as he gets close enough for me to touch and then lunges for the kill.

I squeal, darting to my left and twisting out of his grasp as I make a run for the living room.

"You can run," he calls out, teasing, "but you can't hide."

I bolt through the hallway, wrenching the back door open before he reaches me with his long strides. "Do your best, soldier!"

The grass is dewy underfoot, the first hues of dusk painting the horizon as I run toward the fence line. Slowing to a jog, I turn and trot backward, casing him out. Duke drops off the porch, choosing to keep to a long stride as he bears down on me.

"You make me run, woman, I promise your punishment will be twice as rough." *Why does that sound so good?* "I'm warning you now, I don't like doing any cardio if I don't have to."

I laugh, turning back to face the fence as I zero in on the wooden stile. "Catch me if you can!"

I've got no idea where I'm planning on running to in thick-soled Goth boots. All I know is that I haven't had this much fun in years: fun kicking back and letting go of my inhibitions. Finding the playful side of myself that I quarantined to the dark corners of my mind after Taylah's death.

I took everything that meant happiness and locked it away, afraid that if I showed too much joy in the little things, people would assume that I'd let Taylah go. That I ever could.

My feet swish through the overgrown field as I sprint over the bumpy ground toward the stand of pines at the property line. Duke's heavier footfalls thud behind me, his pace telling me he is, in fact, running. I press on, pumping my legs harder as I laugh like I haven't in a long damn time. It feels good: the burn of the evening air into my lungs, the grass on my legs.

It feels good, that is, until I'm knocked off balance by one hard and heavy body, falling flat on my front, my hands doing little to soften my fall. "Ow!"

I'm rolled to my back, Duke braced over top of me, the muscles in his arms defined as he holds himself clear of my body so he can check me over. "Are you okay? I took you down a bit harder than I expected."

"I guess this is the part where you tell me you were in a rugby team, too?"

"Isn't every Kiwi guy at some point in his life?"

Fair enough. I chuckle, making a move to get out from underneath him, yet he doesn't give me leave to do so. Instead, his elbows bend slightly, his body dropping closer to mine.

"Duke, what are you doing?"

"You need to laugh like that more often," he says quietly, his eyes moving over my face, settling on my lips. "It's a good sound on you."

"*You* need to laugh more often, period." I reach between us, settling my hand gently on his chest, testing the limits.

"How does this work?" he asks, his head dipping down, his breath tickling my face as he talks. "Once the car's fixed—"

"Fuck the car." I let my hand slide to his neck and run my thumb along the underside of his strong jaw. "What does it matter?"

"It gets fixed, I leave," he murmurs. "This ..." He tucks his chin to his chest, seeming to look down at how our bodies touch at the hips. "Us—it won't last."

"Only if you don't want it to." My heart lives in my throat as I search his eyes, looking for the truth. Does he want this? He said I drive him nuts, but isn't love a kind of madness? Could he *love* me, or will I only be a passing phase, a moment of lust, a simple dream?

"I want it too, Cam." Duke's eyes find mine, his throat bobbing hard as he swallows. "But wanting it and getting it are two different things."

"So have what you can now. Don't worry about the future—forget the past. Live this with me. Fuck, just enjoy what we're doing, acting like two teenagers in an overgrown field. How often can you say you've let go and lived, Duke?"

His brow furrows, his eyes darkening the same as the sky does over us. I flex my hand on his neck to hold him here with me, make sure he doesn't slip away to some place I'm not familiar with, a time gone by that I don't know how to find him in.

"Live with me," I whisper, pressing on his nape with my fingertips to urge him closer.

He lets out a heavy sigh through his nose, and then drops his mouth to mine. It's everything our stolen kisses this morning and last night weren't: urgent, needed, hungry. He tilts his head, burying one hand in my hair as he drops to his forearms in the grass. I gasp at the sudden pang as he pulls tight, anchoring me to him and stealing my next breath with his desperate kiss.

I wanted him to need me. I wanted him to save me from myself. But as he closes his eyes tight and pulls away to press his forehead to mine, I wonder who it was our chance meeting rescued from a life sentence of grief?

"It's okay," I whisper, unsure *what* exactly I'm assuring him of.

All I know is that behind those eyes, a battle rages. One that's not fought overseas with guns and tanks, but one that wreaks havoc in the homeland with harshly spoken words and misguided beliefs.

He's so hard on himself, his worst critic, but why?

"You're the first since her," he says through strained tones. "There hasn't been anyone else; never could be."

"The first what?" I loop both arms around his neck, holding him to me, not allowing him to walk away from what we've started here.

"The first woman I've kissed in a long fucking time." He pushes on his hands, breaking my hold as he rears back to kneel between my legs. "I've been back from the war for three years, Cam. Three years, I've stuck to myself. Three years, I lived in limbo, refusing to believe there was anyone else for me."

"What are you talking about?" I push up on my elbows, frustrated that this isn't where our kiss was supposed to lead, but equally intrigued. "*Who* are you talking about?"

"My wife."

His fucking what? "You're married?"

"Was," he murmurs. "She died."

I want to disappear. I feel so ashamed. He's been listening to me break apart these past days, and he's been hiding this? "Duke, I'm sorry. I shouldn't have got riled up like that. I'm ... shit, I don't know what else to say."

His lips tilt up in a sad smile. "I finally silenced you, huh?"

A short, sharp laugh erupts from my chest. "I guess so."

He reaches for my hand, taking it in his and pulling me up so I sit in front of him, my legs splayed in a most un-ladylike fashion on either side of his. "I didn't want to kill the mood, Cam. I'm sorry. It's just ..."

"The reality hit you hard?"

"Yeah." He frowns, tracing my cheek with his fingertip. "I didn't mean to make you feel bad or anything. Hell, you should be proud."

"Proud?" I say with a laugh. "What on earth for?"

"Being the amazing woman you are. I swore off ever dating again, adamant that I'd lost my only chance at being happy. And after that, it just became normal to be on my own, normal to stick to myself. But you ..." He shakes his head, looking down to my lap as he takes my hands in his. "You won't relent. You're in my head even when you're not here."

"I have that effect on people," I tease.

He smiles, lifting his gaze to mine. "Do you believe in fate?"

I nod, the belief that he was placed in my path for a reason so strong I can almost taste it. People don't come into your life without purpose; they always have a role to play. How else could I justify only being given a little less than five short years with Taylah?

"I want to try this," Duke says, shaking my hands gently as though to drive his conviction home. "My gut tells me I'd be stupid to pass you up, even though my heart tells me this can only be trouble."

"Thank you, I guess?" I twist my lips up in an unsure smile. *He was complimenting me, right?*

Duke huffs out a small laugh, moving his hands to my face. "Now let's stop talking and try again, huh?"

He doesn't need to tell me twice. I tilt my head, letting my eyes slip closed as he kisses me again, this time slower and with more purpose. He tells me through his touch that he's for real, that he legitimately wants to see where this leads. He promises with the slow and measured way he coaxes me to lie down that I can back out at any time, no questions asked.

Yet I don't want to. My back hits the grass, and I hook my legs around his hips, my calves pulling him flush against me. Duke holds our kiss as he drops to his forearms again, his chest pressed so tightly against mine that I couldn't mistake the quickened beat of his heart if I tried.

The sun has all but set as he moves those hot lips of his to my jaw, kissing a line down my neck to my shoulder. I tip my head back, ignoring the scratch of the dirt below as I part my lips on a silent moan. His rough hand slides across my collarbone as his lips linger on my jaw, his fingers tucked beneath the edge of my cardigan.

I couldn't pick a more perfect evening: the stars come out to play as the last rays of light die off, the night providing a spectacular backdrop as I look at the man who carefully kisses his way down my body. It's too much, too fast, yet at the same time it feels only natural.

I've never been able to click with someone like I have Duke. Maybe our first day together had teething problems, but the time we've shared since has been easy, natural, comfortable. I don't feel judged when I'm with him, and most importantly, I *trust* him. I don't believe he'd ever intentionally hurt me.

"You with me?" he whispers in gruff tones as he returns to lie over me, his hands either side of my head.

"Wouldn't be anywhere else." I push my shoulders back, reaching up to meet his lips in another stolen kiss.

The rumble in his chest vibrates through my own, a gasp falling from my parted lips as he shunts a hand beneath my butt to press me harder against him. There's no denying how he feels now. None at all.

The grass shrouds us from the moonlight that takes over from the day before, yet it still provides enough light for me to make out the intensity in Duke's eyes as he holds my gaze.

He doesn't have to say anything at all for me to know he's asking permission, asking if this is okay. I rock my hips into his in reply, my bottom lip pinched between my teeth as I urge him to follow through with whatever thought runs through his mind.

"You're fucking gorgeous, you know that?" He searches my eyes, a small furrow in his brow. "But it's not what got to me."

Words fail me as he tucks a hand beneath my loose shirt, and palms my stomach, squeezing my side.

"It's all of you, Cam. They say true beauty lies within, and babe, you've got that in spades." His wrist turns, his fingers edging beneath the waist of my leggings and thong until he cups me in his firm hold. I moan without inhibition as his fingers apply the barest pressure.

"You're going to wreck me," I half-heartedly protest, pushing against his hand to beg for more.

"You ruined me the moment you threw your damn car in reverse, woman."

He splays his fingers, parting me for better access. I'm soaked, and I know it—itching for release at his hand. "Jesus, Cam."

"Totally your fault." I groan as he slides a digit through the wet folds.

Duke doesn't hesitate, his breaths coming quick and heavy as he pushes one, and then two fingers inside of me. He shakes his head as though he can't believe that we're lying out in the field, doing this. Hell, I can't, but it doesn't mean I'm about to halt things. "God you look amazing when you're turned on."

He better shut that mouth of his unless he wants me to come already. My chest rises and falls in shallow bursts as he pumps his fingers in and out, flicking my nub with his thumb. "Oh, God ..."

"Good?" His voice is husky and raw as he leans down to steal a chaste kiss.

"Best," I pant, wriggling to get my hips closer to his hand.

He pushes harder, faster, laying hot kisses across my neck and chest as he does. My muscles tighten, causing him to rear back and slow his pace.

"Don't stop," I beg, anticipating the release I know is about to hit.

"It's okay," he assures me. "I won't stop. Just wanted to see your face when you come."

Fuck me. It's all he has to say. My back arches off the ground, my thighs clamping down hard on his arm as he thrusts his hand hard to finish me off.

I was right. So right.

This man has totally wrecked me.

"Fucking gorgeous," he mutters before pulling his hand free to lick his fingers clean.

So wrecked. I close my eyes with a satisfied sigh as my body sags back against the ground. I choose to lie there and revel in the rush that still pulses through my body a little longer before even considering returning the favour.

As my breaths even out and my climax-induced euphoria dies off, it dawns on me that Duke's fallen deathly quiet.

I open my eyes, expecting to find him watching me, waiting. But I don't.

My heart picks up pace for an entirely different reason when I find instead, Duke still kneeling between my legs, only his focus isn't on me anymore.

"Duke? Everything okay?" I push up on my elbows, scooting back so I can shift to my knees, same as him.

He doesn't answer; his eyes are hard, his brow pinched as he stares off into the dark field beyond.

"What is it?" I whisper, searching the grass for whatever he's seen. "Duke? Talk to me." *What the hell is he looking at?*

His gaze slides back to mine, but I'm met with an entirely different man to the one who made me forget where I was mere seconds ago. His jaw clenches, his throat bobbing as he swallows.

Yet still, he says nothing.

"Duke, you're scaring me."

What have I done?

TWENTY-ONE

DUKE

"Duke. You're scaring me."

Cammie's eyes go wide as she starts to back away from where I kneel frozen in my fear. *I've ruined her.* Wrecked what we had before it started.

"Cam ..."

"Thank Christ," she sighs. "Talk to me, would you?"

I pat the pockets of my jeans, ignoring my rapidly deflating hard-on, and pull my phone out. Slamming my finger across the screen, I switch the torch on and lay it between us.

"What's going on?" Her gaze flicks from the phone to me, before her face falls.

I see the puzzle come together in her softened eyes: my fear of sleeping in the open, the fact I make sure she goes to bed before me, the fact this isn't the first time I've used my phone as a torch when it wasn't really necessary.

"You're afraid of the dark," she says on a whisper.

I've never told anyone, and for good reason. What kind of a man is crippled by a fear that only small children keep?

My mum—she knows about the nightmares. My brother—he knows I don't sleep well, but not why. At home, my bed is pushed into a corner of the room with no windows adjacent, the tallboy beside the bed so it boxes me in. At home, I cope, however miserably.

"I didn't think when we left the house."

"It's okay." She scoots forward, setting her hands on my thighs.

The simple gesture grounds me, the basic action of her touch doing so much for me right now that I don't think she could possible comprehend how amazing she is. I literally made this woman come and now I'm an anxious mess, yet all she thinks about is how *I* feel.

"I'm sorry." She opens her mouth to say something in return, yet I silence her with a raised hand. "I know. Pathetic, huh?" God, what does she think of me? "I wasn't always like this."

Lame comeback, Duke.

"Since the incident overseas?" she asks, her hands massaging my thighs.

I nod. "It was night time when they attacked. I guess the fact they caught us off guard, hit the place by surprise, triggered something in my subconscious. I've been told by doctors in the past that my brain made a connection to the fear of the attack and the fact it was during the night. That's why I'm afraid now when it's not light; I can't see the threat my brain tells me *should* be there."

"Ghosts," she whispers. "You were looking for ghosts from your past."

"Pretty much."

Cam takes my phone in her hand, careful not to

obstruct the light. She rises to her feet, one hand outstretched toward me. I take it, allowing her to coax me up as well.

"We can't keep doing this," she says as she guides us toward the house. "Letting our pasts dictate who we are today."

"How do you change everything about who you are, though?" She has a life outside of her fear to feed off, to give her strength. Me? All I am is the broken vet who can't hold down a job to save himself.

"One step at a time." She nods, resolute in her answer.

All I can do is squeeze her hand in reply. There aren't any words that could adequately voice how thankful I am to have found her. She's done what others couldn't, and all without a second thought or the slightest ounce of frustration.

I've only ever known one other woman like that, and the fleeting thought that someday, I could lose this one, too, threatens to have me sitting immobile once more.

I couldn't go through that again. Never.

"Well," Cammie says, breaking the silence between us, "I had fun for the most part. What about you?" She laughs, cementing the fact I don't deserve her. What have I done to merit this kind of unwavering happiness in my life?

I tug on Cam's hand, bringing her to a stop so I can swing her to face me. Her smile shows nothing but a genuine ability to look for the best in the situation. "Unwanted panic attack aside, I think we can agree we both had a good time."

She tilts her chin up as I lean down to take her lips

with mine. Her kisses are a salve I can never have too much of.

"I'm thinking," she says with a grin as we resume our trek to the house, "since we've wasted a whole heap of time running around like two raucous kids, how about we start the diet another day and have pancakes for dinner?"

I huff out a laugh as I smile, hanging my head between my shoulders. "You're really something, you know that?"

"I've been told." Cam bats her eyelashes. "Come on. Admit it: you're secretly excited at the idea of a sugar-overloaded feel-better-now dinner."

Not particularly. My gut churns simply thinking about all that syrup and butter. "How about I just cook again? It can be my way of paying board."

"Deal." She snaps her fingers. "My rear end has already gained a kilo thinking about all that refined sugar, anyway."

I bark out a laugh while pulling my hand from hers and promptly slapping it across her arse. "This thing is hardly fat, woman."

"It's hardly size small, either."

"It's sexy," I insist. For fuck's sake, I've barely been able to keep my eye off the thing. "You women and your bodies."

"Come on," she exclaims. "Men can hardly critique how harsh us women are on our bodies when it's *your* gender that set unrealistic expectations of what 'pretty' is."

"Fuck me," I groan. Knew she was too good to be true. "Don't tell me you're a feminist as well."

"I prefer realist. You can't deny that there's a real inequality when it comes to the expectations society sets on women over men. I mean, it's totally accepted for an overweight guy to score a hot, fit young woman, right? But if an overweight woman bags herself a hot, fit young guy, she's suddenly a cougar, or he's a chubby-chaser. It's bullshit."

"I don't know," I say on a sigh as I guide her up the stile. "All I know is that if a woman has hips and tits, then the primal part of a man can't help but notice. Cut it whichever way you like, but men are built to hunt and provide, and they're attracted to the fact women are built to breed and care for the young."

"Yeah?" Cam says quietly. "Well, some of us obviously failed at the breeding and caring part." She storms off ahead as I hustle over the stile with my foot in my goddamn mouth.

What the fuck was I thinking saying that? *Douche, Duke. Fucking douche move, that was.* "Shit, Cam. I didn't mean that."

She shakes her head, pushing on ahead.

"Cam." I jog to catch up, determined to fix this. "Wait up, would you?"

"I'm sorry," she blurts as she stops and turns to face me. "It's just ... you struck a chord, you know? You're right to a degree, and that's what hurts. I'm a woman, and yet I'm a shit mum." Her brow twitches. "I *was* a shit mum."

God, no. Never. I take her shoulders in my hold and bend a little to level our gazes. "You are *not* a shit mum."

"How can you say that when my negligence caused

my daughter's death? Do you have any idea how many different ways I could have stopped what happened? I could have locked the door before I dozed off; I could have put up with the blocked sinuses and just dealt with it; I could have waited until Jared got home to feel sorry for myself and wallow in my head-cold-induced misery. Jesus, Duke, the list never ends."

"No, it doesn't. But what the fuck does beating yourself up over again and again achieve now?" I ask.

She stares into my eyes, her brow hard as she seems to search for something—who knows what? A sign that I'm lying, telling her what she needs to hear?

Not going to find it.

"Answer me, Cam." I give her shoulders a gentle shake. "What the fuck does any of that achieve now? Can you go back and change what happened?"

"No." She pouts.

"Does hindsight help you deal with the grief at all?"

"Well, no, but—"

"Exactly." I drop my hands to my sides and straighten up. "So let it go. You were no more able to foresee what would happen when you took those drugs than I was when I re-deployed thinking I'd still have a wife when I got back."

"So why do you still beat yourself up over the past as well, Duke?"

Damn. She's nailed it on the head with that question. Why *do* I blame myself for not being able to do more after the attack, for not being able to stop my wife driving that day? I couldn't prevent either of those events any more than she could prevent hers. What *would* one more scorned soldier running off into the desert with a loaded weapon, or being home the day family died, have achieved?

It wouldn't have changed what happened, that's for sure.

It may have been her daughter's door we opened last night, but as I look at Cam patiently waiting on me to answer, it becomes obvious that it was never her issues we were bringing into the light.

It was mine.

This was never meant to be about me.

"Come inside, Duke." Cam holds her hand toward me, her head cocked slightly to the side. "Let's go eat. My stomach thinks my throat's been cut."

"You go ahead; I'll be in soon."

Her eyes narrow. "You don't like the dark."

"I know that, Cam," I snap a little too harshly given how she whips her head back. "Perhaps I feel like a good old shock to the senses might help."

I can't explain it, but the way she turned the conversation around, pointed out that my observations about her inability to cope come from having the same faults in myself, makes me want to face this last demon head on.

"Now isn't the time." Her fingers thread in mine. "We can deal with this one together, later."

"I've got to do it—face my fears," I say, turning back to face her. "Like you said, we can't keep living like this."

"No, we can't. But like I also said," she says, "we have to change our habits one step at a time.'

I don't answer her, my focus on the dark fence line, the trees, and the parts of the yard that are blackest of all. Somewhere out there is danger. Somewhere out there is the ghost of my past waiting to be banished for good.

"I'm reverting back to the original idea of pancakes," Cam states. "With maple syrup."

Now isn't the time to do this, Duke. "Jam," I answer. "Do you have jam?"

She giggles, handing me my phone and tugging me toward the house. "Jam is for pikelets, silly."

"Is a pancake not an over-sized pikelet?"

She lifts her eyebrow as her mouth twists in thought. "I suppose you're right."

I gesture for her to go inside first as I switch the torch off and pocket my shame for later. "Thank you."

Cam glances back over her shoulder as we make our way up the hall. "For what?"

"Not making fun of me."

"Why on earth would I do that?" Cam says as she busies herself pulling ingredients from the pantry.

I retrieve a mixing bowl and whisk, heading to the fridge for milk. "A guy my size, my age, scared of the dark?" I snort. "Don't tell me you didn't laugh a little on the inside. You were probably disgusted you let a wimp like me touch you."

"Nope." She measures flour and then baking powder as I try to figure her out. "I might have felt sorry for you when I worked out why you flipped like that, but I don't pity you."

"Why not?" Isn't that human instinct? To pity those weaker than yourself?

"Because, Duke, pity is what you feel when someone is pathetic and unable to help themselves. You're neither of those things."

"You barely know me," I say setting the milk down and leaning a hip into the counter.

"I know enough to let you touch me." She taunts me with my own words as she adds the final ingredients to her bowl and then whisks it into a smooth batter.

I hold my position as she moves around me, warming the skillet and pouring the first pancake in to cook. Her focus is on the batter as it bubbles, but the look in her eye says she's about as mentally present in this room as I am.

Less than a week, and this woman has managed to steamroll a path through my bullshit to rip the core of my issues wide open. I can't change, can't fix myself if I continue to hide the worst of me and pretend I'm doing okay.

I'm not okay. I'm a fucking mess, and while I clearly acknowledge that, I also keep those around me at a protective arm's length. My mum? Shit, she's done nothing but stand by my side, and what have I done for her in return? Become as much of an emotionally shut-off arsehole as my old man.

All in the name of "saving face". What good is it, though, upholding this ridiculous ideal that real men don't cry if inside it's breaking me apart and turning me into a bitter man who's on a fast track to a life lived alone in a forest cabin, spitting at anyone who dares step foot on his property?

I've got to let her in, show her my weaknesses knowing that she's so far proven to be the kind of person who won't take advantage of them. I've got to try and make this work between us. I have to let go in order to hold on.

"You've got your show tomorrow, yeah?"

Cam looks up from plating another fluffy pancake on the stack, and shakes her head. "No, Thursday. Tomorrow I'm doing a fundraising event, remember? That's why we're supposed to be eating healthy, because I won't have much time for dinner between leaving work and getting there." She snorts a supressed laugh.

"Can I come?"

Her eyebrows lift as she carefully answers, "If you want to. I mean, I didn't think that would be your thing, but if you're sure. I could probably put you to good use. They always need people to help corral the kids when they get overexcited and out of hand."

"Kids?"

"Kids." A soft smile spreads across her lips. "It's the annual disco at the kindergarten."

"Kids *and* dancing?" Kill me now ..."

"Aw, Duke. You're not afraid of a few ankle-biters, are you?"

"Of course not. I'm just ... I don't know many people with kids, so I'm not that good with them." I was never gifted the chance to see my own.

"You were one once, right?" She gives the remaining batter another stir while continuing to smirk at me.

"You're not going to make this easy on me, are you?"

"Never." She wiggles her eyebrows and returns to cooking the pancakes.

Subject closed. *Damn it.*

I set the table for us as she finishes the last of the batter, reminding myself that I'm at T-minus approximately five days and counting. Maybe if I tell the therapist that I stepped outside my comfort zone and helped a woman I just met with kids, they'll go easy on the exercises they give me? *Unlikely.* Still, letting them know that I volunteered to help at a kindergarten disco can't be—

Shit. "Is this fundraiser at night?"

"Well, yeah. I said it's after work." Cam's eyes go wide as she dumps the empty batter bowl in the sink. "Oh. I'm sure it'll be fine, though, Duke. Heaps of lights and plenty of people around to reassure you everything's okay." She looks about as convinced as I feel.

"I thought you meant it was a late afternoon thing. I didn't think it through properly before I offered." *Idiot.*

"The dark is a hard limit for you, huh?" She doesn't ask to criticise; her tone tells me she's genuinely concerned.

"Can be a pain in the arse, yeah."

"How do you cope, normally?"

I laugh bitterly as she sets the stack down on the table. "I don't—clearly."

"You know what? Don't worry about it." Cam takes her seat. "Stay here and kick back. I'm sure it'll only be a couple of hours, tops. You can pick out a movie for us to watch when I get home or something."

"If you're sure?" *Quitter.*

She sighs, holding my gaze across the table with her fork poised over her plate. "Small steps, remember? I'm thinking a crazy busy kindergarten car park that's lit up with only a few strings of fairy lights probably won't be the best idea. You might get a few funny looks if you're wandering around with your phone out like you're about to take pictures. You know, some strange guy with no kids of his own there and all." She laughs it off as a joke, but it's anything but. It's my life: the story of a fully-grown man who can't attend a harmless fundraiser because it's at night, and it involves kids.

All the reminders of what I lost rolled into one.

Some hero ...

TWENTY-TWO

CAMMIE

"Oh, Cammie. I'm so glad you're here. I had a couple of mums lined up to help me get the tables set out, but one's stuck in the traffic, and the other has a son who won't stop vomiting." The manager of the kindergarten, stands with her arms full of streamers and her eyes full of panic.

"Point me in a direction, Jacinda, and I'll have them laid out in no time."

"You're a lifesaver."

I set my bag down with the boxes of decorations and activity supplies and get to work laying out the trestle tables in the closed off car park. By the time the sun goes down and the parents return with their children, we have six stations set up with various activities for the kiddies to try out to get spot prizes and crafts to take home. I get comfortable at my face-painting station as Jacinda rushes past again, a huge tub of swollen water balloons in her hands.

"Have you got everything you need?"

"I think so." I do a quick glance over the table, cataloguing the brushes, paints, and accessories.

"If you need anything, flag down one of the girls to get it for you." Her shoulders drop as her face softens, and I know, I just know, she's about to do it. "You know, it really is amazing that you still help us out."

She doesn't have to say it. The unspoken words hang in the air between us. *"Even though your daughter doesn't come here anymore."*

"I honestly don't mind." I offer her a smile, hoping she'll drop the subject and leave.

To be honest, I think the heavy tub in her hands is probably the reason she chooses to drop the conversation and carry on, but either way, I'm happy she does.

I started out helping with the fundraiser partially as a way to say thanks to the girls for the great care they gave Taylah, but mostly to prove to myself and the community that even though the headlines dumped the reason for our daughter's death squarely on me, I wasn't the cold-blooded monster the write-ups made me out to be. That I could still be useful, helpful, and a welcome face in our town.

Now I'm stuck in a catch twenty-two. If I keep going, people look at me with the pity I spoke to Duke about, thinking, *"Poor old, Cammie. Can't find it in herself to let go."* But at the same time, if I stop, then I get the flipside with people thinking I don't care anymore. *"You know her heart was never really in it, don't you?"*

So here I sit, sponging white paint over a child's face with a smile while on the inside I'm in turmoil over what I should do next year. What's worse, I hate letting people down, and I could almost guarantee if I tell Jacinda this is it, disappointed is how she'll react.

"Hey, Cammie."

I look up from the skeleton I'm working on to find Archie standing in line with his little girl. "Oh, hey, Archie. How are things going at the workshop?"

"Part's on its way for your houseguest, so he should be out of town soon enough."

Totally not what I meant, but okay. "He'll be pleased to hear that." Although I can't deny the rush of panic that sends my heart into a flutter when I think about Duke leaving.

"Think you could do us a wee butterfly, here?" he asks. "I've just seen a guy I need to talk to about some mods."

"Yeah, sure." I offer him a smile as I darken the under eye of the boy in my chair. "I'll keep an eye on this little ratbag." Archie's girl giggles as I reach out and tickle her belly.

"Thanks, Cammie."

Thanks, Cammie. Thanks, Cam. Thanks, thanks, thanks.

The word cycles in my head, irritating the hell out of me. It's never really struck me before, but I hear it so often because, at the end of the day, I do so much for everyone. Not that I mind being thanked. I mean, it's common courtesy to show your appreciation when a person helps you out. But for the first time, as I paint obtuse triangles to make my skeleton's cheeks appear sunken, I realise I hardly ever say it myself.

And a girl's got to ask herself, why is that?

Because how often does anyone return the favour?

"Are you done?"

I snap my focus back to the boy in the chair as he

looks up at me sitting there with my brush mid-stroke. "Almost, honey."

No wonder I'm finding myself so easily taken by Duke—aside from my mother, he's the first person to try to help me without any expectation of reward, and, well, family doesn't count really.

I finish up the skeleton and send him on his way, rinsing my brush off as I usher Archie's girl into the seat. "A butterfly, right?"

She gives me a huge gap-toothed grin. "Yeah. Purple and pink, please."

"With manners like that? Of course."

I start into her art, outlining the wings as I catch glimpses of other people here tonight. Most of them I know in one way or another, from school, through my parents, or acquaintances of mine and Jared's who drifted away after the separation. I know these people, would have gone as far as to call them friends once, but when it comes down to it, I guess you find out who your true pals are in times of crisis.

When I needed them most, who did I have? The girls here dropped by a few times in the first couple of weeks after Taylah's death, but now that I think about it, how much of that was obligation? I don't see Jacinda outside of these functions; she doesn't pop over for a wine, or ask me around to her place. So many friendly faces in this town, but not many *actual* friends.

"Should we add some white spots on the wings?" Perhaps if I convince this child in front of me I'm invested in the lop-sided butterfly, I might convince myself, too.

"You need another antennae."

I follow the outstretched finger up the thick forearm to the even thicker bicep and the man attached.

"Are you okay?" Not my finest greeting, I'm aware.

"I think so," Duke answers with a smile. "I'm here, aren't I?"

I chuckle as he mimics the line I gave him the night we first met.

"How *did* you get here, though?" It's dark out; he would have had to walk. Those two things don't compute.

Duke thumbs over his shoulder to my meddling mother, who's failing in her attempt to look engrossed in Mrs Aitchison's conversation and not as though she's watching us.

I lean out around Duke and poke my tongue out at her. She gives me a cute little finger wave. *Cow.*

"Did she call you, or did you call her?" I ask Duke as I return to fixing the butterfly. "There. All done, sweetheart."

"Thanks, Cammie."

I manage to stave off the hug and restrict it to a pat on the shoulder so that her butterfly doesn't turn into a Picasso tribute on my shirt.

"I called her," Duke answers as he drops into the vacant seat.

I giggle at the sight of him crammed on a kids chair, his knees up around his ears. "Let me guess. Spiderman?"

He wrinkles his nose at the idea. "Nah. Set of lips, right here." He taps his cheek with a thick finger.

"Whatever rocks your boat, I guess." I rinse the brush and go to dip it in the red paint when he stops me.

"Not painted."

What?

"Set of lips, babe. Right here."

Oh, I get it now. *Oh.*

I lean in and place my mouth to his cheek, dotting a gentle peck on his unbelievably sharp stubble.

He makes a throaty grumble as he rests a hand on my knee. "Better."

"You're amazing, you know that? For coming out tonight."

He chuckles, reaching around me to scoot my chair closer to his. "I admit I faked being on Facebook most of the car ride here so I could light up the interior. But it wasn't as bad as I thought."

"Any bad guys jump out of the bushes yet?"

His face falls, his eyes hardening. "It's not a joke."

"And I'm not kidding," I say with a straight face, doing my best to un-wedge my foot from my mouth. "I want to know if I need an escort to my car later."

He smiles, seeming to pick up on my regret, and reaches out to tap the underside of my chin with his finger. "I think you'll be okay."

As much as I love this sudden turnaround back to the cute and cuddly Duke, I can't fight the need to look around and check who watches. What will they think? This guy rocks up in our town a few days ago, and here I am, getting up close and personal already? Shit—what if the gossip gets back to Jared? The arsehole would use that against me in a heartbeat.

"What's the matter?" Duke leans back, his hand sliding off my leg.

"It's not that I'm embarrassed—"

"But I'm being too forward around your friends," he finishes with an ache in his tone.

"They're not my friends—that's just it." I glance over at Jacinda, who lifts a hand in acknowledgement. "I don't know who to trust, who has my best intentions at heart."

"These people love you," he says, as though surprised I would think otherwise. "When I came into town the other day on my own, you were all they could talk about. 'Oh, you're staying with Cammie,'" he mimics. "'You two will get along great'. 'She'll enjoy the company. Such a lovely girl, that she is.'" He twitches a quick smile. "Even got another warning from your cousin."

I chuckle at the voices he puts on, imagining the old ladies around town giving him their two cents' worth, not to mention my overzealous relatives. "I'm sorry about him. He's just protective since Jared left me how he did."

"Oh, no," he says with a chuckle. "It wasn't just him. Archie was another who passively told me he'd rip me apart if I was an arsehole to you."

"Great." I roll my eyes. "So you're just being nice because you're scared of a mechanic and a cop."

"Hardly. I'm being nice because I want the car fixed and to stay out of jail in the meantime." He winks, a playful grin on his heavenly lips.

A little girl steps in between us, which is quite the feat given our proximity. "Can I be a puppy?"

"You can be whatever you want, sweetheart," Duke tells her as he vacates the seat. "I'll hang around with your mum until you're done," he says, backing away.

"Sure. Don't let her chew your ear off, though."

He chuckles, fading into the darkened car park. "Nah, that's your job."

I end up painting Spiderman, not once, but five times. Still, the smiles on the kids' faces when they check themselves out in the hand mirror I have on standby make it totally worth it. The crowd thins out relatively fast, and by eight the car park is empty save for those of us left behind to clean up. Small bonuses that come with volunteering at a children's event—early finish times.

"If you want to head off, I can finish up here," Jacinda offers as I rinse out the paint pots under the outdoor tap.

"Are you sure?"

She grins, jerking her chin to indicate over my shoulder. "Babe, if any man can put up with your mother for that long, he deserves to take you home early."

I look behind me and find Duke watching us as, sure enough, my mother chews his ear off.

"Who is the guy, anyway? He's cute."

A pang of irritation spikes in my chest at the way she blatantly eye-fucks him. "I'll catch up with you later in the week, huh?" I shove the pots into her grasp. "You can tell me how much you managed to raise tonight."

"Sure thing." She wriggles on the spot. "Here he comes, Cam. Like I said—cute."

I restrain from flipping her the bird as she walks away. I've never felt this possessive over a man, not even Jared, and to be frank, it scares me. He's been here all of four days ...

"Ready to go home?"

... and I'm ready to rake my nails over the guy to lay claim. "Sure. Let me grab my bag."

Duke lifts his hand to show the tote slung in his grasp. "Already got it."

"I better say goodnight to Mum."

"She's gone already."

Well, that was quick ... "I guess I'm all done here then," I announce with a quick flap of my arms.

And yet, I don't move.

I knew Duke was hot the minute I first laid eyes on him. I knew he'd be a handful when I invited him to stay. Hell, I knew he'd get under my skin when he first criticised where I keep my coffee. But damn, I never expected to be blindsided with feelings for him like I have been.

I can't move, can't make that first step toward home because I know what'll happen when we get there.

He'll offer to make me a hot drink before bed. I'll have a shower where I'll think about him to the point that I'll consider the logistics of sneaking my vibrator into the bathroom with me next time. He'll strip down to only his sweatpants while he waits on me to go to bed, and the whole time I'll be wondering how long I should wait before making another move so that I don't come off as desperate, hoping he'll spare me the torture by doing it first.

I think a fire walk would be less stressful right now.

"You kind of need to show me where you parked," he coaxes.

"Right." Get in the car and get him home where it's

lit up like a damn Christmas tree. The man doesn't like the dark. He's bound to get uncomfortable if we're still standing here when Jacinda turns the fairy lights off.

Duke reaches out, taking my hand. "It's supposed to be me who's freaking out, remember?"

"Are you?" I put one foot after the other and somehow manage to remember how to walk.

"Not too bad." He squeezes my hand as we head out of the kindergarten car park. "Heart rate's elevated, my subconscious is chatty, but I'm managing to keep a lid on it so far."

"I'm so proud of you for coming tonight."

"Gee, thanks, Cam," he teases.

"No, really." I tug his hand as we near the side street I parked on. "I am proud of you. I gave you an out, and yet you still came. Why?"

"It was important." He shrugs, as though to dismiss the subject.

But I don't want to let it go. I want to know why staying here with me, a woman he's known less than a week, has finally given him the strength to face this fear of his?

"Can we talk about where this thing with us is at?" I pull my hand free as we approach the BMW.

He hastily pulls his phone out as soon the street lights end, and yet he doesn't turn it on; he palms it, turning it over in his hand.

"What do you want to discuss?" The second I unlock the car he's in the front seat quicker than an excited dog.

I drop down into the driver's seat and twist to set my bag in the back. "Was our ... fooling around some heat-of-the-moment thing? A once-off?"

The level at which I'm able to keep my emotions at check seriously impresses me. Normally, I avoid conversations such as this because they're too hard. If I can deny, deny, deny, then that's what I'll do.

And yet, here I am, watching Duke, cool as a cucumber while he formulates a careful answer.

"It might have been heat-of-the-moment, but it wasn't a mistake, Cam. You know that.'

"But?" I sense his hesitancy.

"But, we're fucking strangers, right?" He laughs awkwardly as I start the car. "Don't you think what we did in your paddock was kind of putting the horse before the cart?"

I roll my eyes, gunning the car into the street. "I hardly asked you to marry me, Duke. It was a bit of light groping."

"I finger-fucked you."

"You wanted to," I blurt out in an attempt to ignore the fire those words have ignited in me. "Besides, you were the one who pulled me onto your boner yesterday morning. So that's twice now that you've instigated things."

"You looked hot." He dismisses the fact as though it's self-explanatory why I should accept a rock-hard dick being pressed against me as part of a normal morning routine. "Isn't it normal for a guy to get a hard-on when there's a good looking woman that close to him?"

"You'd think so, but I can name one guy who didn't find me that appealing."

Duke twists in his seat to face me, a frown visible in the dim confines of the car.

"Jared," I confirm what he's no doubt thinking. "My ex. The one who visited the other day."

He keeps staring, his eyes moving up and down my body as I drive.

"What?"

"Just trying to figure out how exactly he could wake up next to you and not get a morning wood."

"I can't believe we're having this conversation."

"You started it."

I look across at him as I bring the car to a stop at one of the few sets of lights in our town. He grins back, and the two of us fall apart laughing at the direction our "serious" chat has gone.

"How on earth did we go from 'What's up with us?' to 'What kind of guy doesn't get a boner in the morning?'" I ask with a laugh.

Duke shrugs, scooting down in his seat to prop one boot up on the side of my centre console. "I have no idea, but it's a legitimate question. Was the guy impotent or something?"

"We had a daughter, remember?" It saddens me how easily I stated that, how relatively unaffected I am referring to Taylah in conversation.

One step at a time.

"True that." He sighs, staring out the window. "I don't know what to say about last night, Cam, other than I liked it and I've been trying to work it out for myself all day. All I know are three things: one, I'm only here a few more days; two, I already miss you when you're not in the house; and three, that doesn't change the fact your funny habits drive me insane."

"You miss me?" I grip the steering wheel a little

tighter as we accelerate onto the stretch of open road before home.

"Yeah." He rolls his head on the rest in my periphery. "It's quiet, and although I normally love the quiet, I think that's because I never knew how good it was to have somebody around who drowns out the bullshit noise in my head."

"I thought you were a hothead," I admit, peering over at him every so often from the corner of my eye. "You lost it at me for asking what the army is like, and I thought you were an arrogant arsehole who needed to calm the hell down."

He chuckles, his hand tapping his leg.

"What?"

"You thought *that* was me losing my temper?"

Oh, damn. "Was it not?"

"Nope." He laughs, nudging my leg with a loose fist. "It's okay, Cam. I'm sure you'll never see that side of me. I've got to get pretty damn pissed off to lose it completely."

"It's not funny, you know. That kind of temper is the sort of thing you said split up your parents."

"Good thing I'm not married anymore then." He scoots up in his seat as we approach the house. "My temper is the reason why I went into the army to begin with," he admits. "Somebody told me I was just like my old man at my age, and that messed me up. I wanted a valid outlet for my rage, a way to get rid of the fact I was nineteen and pissed off at the world. I didn't want to be him."

"Did it work? I would have thought the regiment of daily life would have made your anger worse, considering you'd need to keep it in check most of the time."

"It worked at first. I threw myself into working out and staying not only physically but mentally fit."

"And then?"

"Decked a fellow soldier for harassing one of the local women on our first tour in Iraq."

I bring the car to a stop in the driveway, the lights inside the house beckoning me to bed. But this progress is more important. Infinitely so. "What happened then?"

Duke continues to relax in the seat, staring straight out the windscreen as he talks. "Luckily for me, it happened when we were off-duty, so I got away with a warning. The meathead I punched in the face didn't get so much as a fucking talking to. There was evidence of what I did—his face—but nothing of what he had done to instigate it."

"Well, I bet the woman appreciated what you did."

He chuckles. "Not sure. She ran away screaming something in her language. Poor bitch probably thought we were arguing over who was going to have her first."

Possibly, but still. He defended the honour of a woman he didn't know.

"Come." I open my door to get out.

"Can I turn my torch on now?" His whispered question stills me.

This whole time he's held off, even when he's been freaking out? "Of course. We'll probably need it anyway."

I round the car to his side and wait for him to get his phone sorted out. White light spills over the gravel driveway as I lead us away from the house.

"Where are we going, Cam?"

"I want to show you something." I offer him my hand for support, glad when he takes it.

He follows dutifully beside as I lead him back down the drive to the gateway at the road. I come to a stop a few feet back from the road's edge and take a deep breath. Listening to Duke share his history, the things that make him tick, it's inspired me. If he can face his nightmares head on, dissect and work out what it is about those memories that tear him apart, then why can't I?

"You know how you told me you fear the dark because of its connection to when you were hurt?"

"Yeah."

"It took me almost a year before I could leave the house at dusk. That hour between sundown and night is the most beautiful of the day, I reckon, but for so long what the shades of orange and hints of purple represented scared the ever-loving shit out of me. I couldn't come down here, on foot or in the car, for so long."

"Because that's when she died." Duke takes a step closer, looping an arm around my shoulders and tucking me to his side.

I nod, and then point to a rough patch of grass where the bitumen has chipped, the layers from repeated resealing of the road visible. "That's where the woman hit her." I turn in his hold, taking him with me, and point out a rose bush planted slightly offset from the letterbox. "That's where she landed."

"Cam, you don't have to do this."

"I do." My nose tingles, my eyes sore as the pressure builds within my ears. I fight the tears because after all, what have they ever brought me? Certainly not relief. "I want you to understand, Duke, that nightmares happen in the brilliance of the day as well as the dark of night. A tragic incident is something we can't foresee. Even though we beat ourselves up over the details that are so freaking obvious afterward, there's nothing anyone can do to prevent a true tragedy. Living life afraid of the what-ifs is letting death win before you've even reached the final act."

His chest rises with his deep breath. "You ever feel like you're on this hamster wheel where no matter how fast you run, how much you tire yourself out trying to get ahead, you're still stuck in that same rut?"

"Every goddamn day," I say. "Jared used to tell me that if I bothered to stop and take a breath, I might find that I was actually able to breathe. He thought I would work myself into a frenzy as a charade, a way to prove to people I actually felt guilty for what I did. In his head, I didn't really care. Because he blames me, he can't see how it was possible for me to be affected by Taylah's death. He thought I did it all for show: constant volunteering, working overtime, offering to help people shift house, redecorate—anything that would keep me busy." I rest my head back against Duke's arm and stare over the tree line at the stars beyond. "Truth is, I tried to stop and breathe a few times, but I never felt like there was any air left for me. Instead, my chest would ache as though I was taking on water, drowning in my grief. As long as I found a way to keep busy, I found a way to tread water and stay afloat. I found a way to live."

"And now?" Duke asks gently.

"Now, staying busy is my hamster wheel. Only my wheel is suspended over a black ocean of every mistake I've ever made, and if I falter, I'll drown."

His arm cinches tighter, pulling me close enough that he lays a gentle kiss to my head. "Seems we're both as tethered to our past as each other."

I huff a short, bitter laugh. "Want to cut the cord with me?"

Duke pulls me flush against him, wrapping me inside his strong, warm arms as he rests his chin atop my head. "Woman, I'd dive into the black and drown with you, because for once, I don't think I'd be afraid if you were with me."

TWENTY-THREE

DUKE

"ARE YOU SURE YOU WANT TO DO THIS?" CAM asks as I stand at the foot of her bed.

"Seems only logical given what we did last night."

She presses her lips together, clearly not convinced but willing to let me do what it takes to move on. "How do you want to start?" Her gaze settles on my bare chest, on the scars I carry.

"Lying down." I lift my eyebrows and chuckle with her. She's so cute when she laughs.

"Come on then." Cam pats the mattress with a smile.

I take a deep breath and climb on, crawling up the bed to where she sits. "You know, any time you're not okay with this, just tell me."

"If I wasn't okay with it," she says, tracing a line between my abs with her finger, "I would have laughed at you when you first brought it up."

After she took me down the driveway to share that most intimate detail with me, Cam and I returned to the house to go through our usual nightly routine. She showered, I changed, and we looked awkwardly at each other in the mirror as we brushed our teeth.

Knowing we could do this dance forever, and that our time together is short, I bit the bullet and brought the subject up: why not share the same bed?

"How do you like it?" she asks as I settle on my side, my head propped on my hand to watch her.

"I usually start out on my back, but most of the time face down is better."

"Same." She nudges me in the side with a loose fist. "See? Look at us being best buddies again."

I laugh, reaching out and pulling her to me. "Naw. My bestie."

Cam squeals as I rub her head with my fist, giving her a noogie. "Duke. Stop it."

I do, but only so I can roll to my back and take her with me. She's all kitted out in a sensible pyjama set: skulls with bows on their heads adorn her pink-flocked flannelettes. I pinch the soft fabric between my fingers.

"These really are a tease, you know. A woman could get herself in trouble wearing flannelette around a red-blooded man like me."

She snorts the most un-ladylike laugh at my sarcasm. "Maybe that was my intention?"

A moment passes where neither of us say a thing. Cam lies on top of me, her fingers making lazy circles in my hair.

"This week's going too fast," I say quietly, reaching for her butt.

She smirks as I take a decent handful and squeeze. "It doesn't have to be just a week. You could stay longer, or come back."

"I've got counselling to start, and a job to find. I need to spend some time with Mum, make up for being such a jerk to her."

She sighs out her nose, her eyes hard. "Guess I better put in more hours and get my dungeon finished, then."

She cracks up laughing as I tickle her sides. "Is that so? You going to lock me up, keep me all for yourself?"

"Is that such a bad idea?" she asks between gasped breaths. "Honestly, Duke, stop tickling me."

I relent, waiting until she's caught her breath to kiss her. "Take a day off," I plead. "Skip work for one day so we can hang out together."

"You want me to pull a sickie?" Her words protest the thought, but her eyes say she's all in.

"Yeah. Show me around, babe. Show me what it is you love about this town."

"It's totally going to look dodgy when I turn up at the show looking fit as a fiddle."

"So, say you had a migraine. How they going to know you're lying?"

"Um," she says, tapping a finger to her lips. "They might know my excuse is bullshit when I'm spotted around town with you."

"We'll make it a mission then." I put on my best authoritarian voice. "Operation Sight-Seer. Your mission is to show me the best parts of Burbank without anyone of note knowing our whereabouts."

She does a lame-as-fuck salute, giggling. "Mission accepted."

"Now put your head on my shoulder and go to sleep, woman, because I want you rested for your big day."

She smiles, yet does as she's told and tucks her head onto my shoulder, her nose brushing my throat ever-so-slightly. I thread my fingers in her hair, pulling my arm away to let the lengths runs through my grasp, and then repeat the action.

"Duke?"

"Yeah, Cam?"

"I'm so glad your brother doesn't know how to pick a good car."

I silently chuckle, keeping the sound trapped in my chest. "Me too."

A few more minutes pass with me stroking her hair, and Cammie seemingly drifting off.

"Can I turn the lamp off? Do you think you'll be okay?" She startles the hell out of me when she speaks again.

Will I be okay? I want to say having her beside me will calm the irrational side of my mind, but I'm not sure. I never had anyone since I got home. I've got nothing to compare this to.

"Flick it off. I can always turn it back on after you go to sleep."

"Okay." Cammie reaches out, clicking the switch on the cord.

My muscles tense, my body stiff beneath her as I remind myself where I am, who I'm with.

"You okay?"

"I think so."

She hums, shifting around so that her arms are tucked under my shoulders, her forearms cradling my head. It's such a simple position, one a person might assume purely to be comfortable, but knowing *why* she does it tears me apart. Her arms give me a false sense of security, make me feel encased and secure. She does it to make me feel better, but what she doesn't realise is that *she* makes me feel better. Not what she does, but who she is.

"Can I ask you a question?" She sounds so unsure of herself, which is rare.

"Of course."

"What was your wife like?" Cam whispers to the dark.

"Are you sure you want to talk about this?"

She moves around on top of me, and even though I can't see her, I know she's propped herself up by the bony elbows digging into my ribs. "I feel as though she's a part of what made you who you are today, and if I want to know the gorgeous man in my bed a little better, I need to understand that aspect of your history as well."

I get what she's saying, but a part of me is reluctant to tell her because that would only open the Pandora's box of pain and confusion I've kept shelved for so long. *If she did it, so can you.*

"We got together the same year I enlisted in the army," I explain. "We were young: I'd literally just turned twenty, and she was nineteen."

"High school sweethearts?"

"No. We met after graduating. Her brother was friends with mine. We didn't date for long before we were married."

"Love at first sight, then?"

"Not quite. I thought if I married her it would tame her jealous streak." I chuckle, recalling the night of my stag do. "Just made her worse. She had a wicked temper when it came to other women and me."

"She loved you." Cam says. "I'd be jealous too."

"That so?" I reach out and run my hands over her head, brushing Cam's hair off her face.

"Mm-hmm." She leans across and flicks the lamp on, a shy smile on her lips as I blink at the light. "I figured we're not trying to sleep anyway."

Doesn't bother me any. At least I can see her now, read her expressions and reactions to the things I tell her.

Cam pushes on my chest to lean forward and place a chaste kiss to my lips. "Carry on."

"There's not much else to say, other than we decided to start a family while I was home between deployments. She was six and half months pregnant when they died."

"Why didn't you say that before?" Cammie frowns. "Duke?"

"Never seemed relevant, given what you went through. I didn't want you to feel as though I was cheapening your loss by comparing it to mine." I run my thumb across her bottom lip as she stares at me, her frown still in place.

"Why would you think that's how I'd feel?"

"Because you knew your daughter," I say. "I didn't meet my son. He didn't have a name until he died with her."

"Doesn't make him any less important," she whispers.

I wipe the tear from her cheek and continue, keen to get this conversation finished and shelved again for another day. "We'd talked the week before, and she was happy; baby was good, she was healthy." I pause when I realise Cam stares at me with a sad smile on her face.

"What?"

"Nothing really. It's just …"

I lift my eyebrows to tell her to explain.

"It's just the look on your face when you talk about her. I can tell you loved her."

She picks her words carefully, but I can still see the uncertainty in her eyes, feel the tension in her body. Yeah, I loved my wife. Still do. But our time together came to an end the day she died, and this fucking ace of a girl lying on top of me needs to know that.

"*Loved* her," I stress. "She'll always be in my heart, but Cam, it's time to move on. I'm ready to find forever in someone else, someone who's here, now."

She can't hide her relief. Cam's cheeks pink as she tucks her chin against me to hide her face behind her hair.

With my thumbs on her jaw, I coax her head up again, holding her gaze. "Talk to me."

"It's nothing."

"It's something," I say, brushing my thumbs across her cheekbones. "Why did you ask me about her, really?"

"I would say it's jealousy, but we both know that's not it."

"So, what is it?"

"Insecurity," she whispers.

I roll to my left, Cam in my arms so that she ends up beneath me. "Why?"

"You loved her," she says simply, watching her finger as she toys with the ends of my hair. "What if I don't compare, Duke?"

She's scared of losing out again, of being burned for

not being enough. *And damn, don't I know how that feels.* It makes me want to know why a woman who should be loved as much as her feels as though she couldn't be. It makes me ask the only logical question. "Why did Jared leave you, Cam?"

"Started fucking his hairdresser," she states, cool and detached. "But that was just the outcome of a long and rocky patch, anyway. We'd been over for at least a year before that."

"So he should have left," I grit out, trying to tamp down my anger. Fuck, he could have walked out when he knew the marriage was over. He didn't have to hurt her unnecessarily like that.

"It's okay," she says with a sad smile. "It's old news."

"It's not okay, Cam." I lean down and kiss her forehead. "It's not okay."

"Can't change the past, right?"

"No. But we can sure enjoy the future." I kiss her slow and careful, threading my fingers through her hair before I pull away.

She watches me with such intensity, such worry. "What *does* our future hold, Duke?"

My dick twitches as she takes her bottom lip between her teeth, her eyes hopeful.

"What do you want it to hold, Cam?" I rock my hardening erection into her, making her aware exactly what the sight of that pinched lip does to me.

She releases the flesh with a pop, pressing her lips together instead, as though doubting herself.

I lean down and kiss the point where her neck curves into her shoulder, running my tongue in a line to her earlobe before whispering, "Tell me."

Cam swallows, her cheeks flushed as she says, "I want you to fuck me, Duke. I don't know where this thing between us leads, but I know one thing for sure." Her hands track a path along my arms, over my shoulders and down my back. "I don't want to be left wondering what might have happened if I wasn't afraid."

"Afraid of what?" I pop the buttons on her pyjama top as we talk, pushing the fabric aside to reveal her full tits. Jesus—they're everything I thought they'd be.

"Of telling you how I feel." She gasps as I take one of her pert nipples between my forefinger and thumb, and pinch.

I can't help myself—I lean down and take the nipple in my mouth, running my tongue around the tight bud and sucking her soft flesh. She whimpers, squirming beneath me and biting down on that fucking lip again as she tries to stifle the sounds she makes.

"There's no need to be quiet, babe," I say. "You can be as loud as you want."

Fuck it all if her nipples don't harden to rock at that suggestion.

"Talk to me, Cam," I say, rocking myself against her so my dick rubs her clit. "How *do* you feel right now?"

She shuts down, her arms twitching as she tries to cover her chest. "I don't want you to think I'm rushing us into this, Duke. I don't want to scare you away."

"Babe," I grumble, "you're so fucking turned on your nipples could cut glass, not to mention the fact I'm about ten seconds away from ripping your fucking pyjamas off so there's nothing between us anymore. You're worried about scaring me off?" I search her eyes, finding only raw lust. "If you can't tell I want this as much as you do, then I don't know what else I can say or do to show you that." I rock against her, pulling a whimper from that sweet mouth. "Get undressed."

She sucks in a sharp breath as I push against the mattress and get off her to do the same. Cam's cheeks stay the perfect shade of pink as she removes her pyjamas, slow and as sensual as you can make it when they're a practical winter set. Not that it matters; she'd look sexy in a paper bag, I'm sure of it.

She drops the clothing off the side of the bed, settling her shoulders back against the headboard. I strip my boxers off and kick them across the floor, then take my dick in my hand and stroke it a few times before re-joining her on the bed. Those crisp blue eyes track my every movement, her legs falling open as I settle between her ankles, sitting back on my heels.

"Every bit as beautiful as I thought you'd be."

The blush in her cheeks grows, and yet, she takes me by surprise when she lifts a hand to her mouth, wets her fingertips, and then promptly begins to play. The sight of her rubbing circles over her mound drives me to take my cock in hand again and lazily pull at the taut flesh as she starts to squirm.

"Fucking beautiful," I whisper as I shift to my stomach to lie with my head between her legs.

Cam slows her play, allowing me to take over when I place two fingers to her pussy and spread her wide. "Can I?"

"Please," she whispers on an exhale.

I shuffle up the bed until I'm so close that I can smell how aroused she is. *And she thought I wouldn't want this?* Is the woman crazy?

A guttural groan echoes around the room as I run the tip of my tongue along the length of her slit. "Fuck, you taste good." Better than anything she could whip up in that kitchen of hers, unless it was Cam spread out naked on her dining table.

"Duke," she murmurs, her eyes closed as she presses her head back into the bed.

"Yeah, babe?" I run my tongue the length of her again, this time finishing with a sneaky flick of her clit.

She damn near bucks me off the bed. "Oh!"

A guy has to assume she's this sensitive because it's been a while since she's had a man's touch. Fuck, I choose to believe that, because the thought of some guy with his hands on her would drive me to fuck her hard and fast, and that's not what I want for us tonight. She has to be cherished, reminded why she deserves better than an asshole who up and left her for his fucking hairdresser.

I slip one finger inside of her, pumping it slowly back and forth, watching her grow glistening wet. "So pretty." Adding another finger, I drive deep, pushing them to the knuckles as I rub her clit with my thumb.

The sounds coming from Cam are nothing short of magic as she wriggles up the bed, her thighs clamping down on my head as I lean in and flick my tongue across her hood. "Duke, I'm going to come if you keep that up."

"Then come, babe." Because I'm sure to have her doing it again in no time.

Her fingers find my hair, her grasp harsh as she clamps her hand down on the back of my head and holds me in place. I thrust harder with my fingers, stopping every so often with them buried deep to curl one toward her G-spot. Cam's muscles tighten, her pussy hot and swollen as I lick the length of her, drinking her taste while she climaxes.

"Fuck, Duke." She throws her head back, those tits pushed out in such a way that I can't help but reach around her leg and take one in my grasp. "Oh, fuck."

I slow my pace, pulling my fingers free of her cunt as she reaches the end of her high. She watches me with sated eyes as I lick them clean, and then stalk up the bed until I'm over top of her.

"I'm telling you now, I'm clean. So it's up to you whether you want me bare or gloved, babe." I already saw the birth control pills in the bathroom.

She hesitates, the indecision clear in the slight furrow of her brow. "Bare always feels better."

I steal her next breath with my kiss, sweeping my tongue around hers before saying, "Damn straight it does."

She pulls in a deep breath, her eyes locked on mine as I lean down and rest my forehead against hers. For a split second, it's everything—the two of us connected in such a way that for a fleeting moment I forget all the shit that happened to bring me to her.

I edge my hips forward, Cam tilting hers to line my cock up with her entrance. She sighs as I edge the tip inside, biting her lip and groaning when I push the rest of myself balls' deep.

Fuck … that's heaven, right there.

"God damn you feel good." I slide out, relishing every twitch her muscles make as I do, and then slam home hard and fast.

She cries out, moaning as I repeat the process a little faster. The harder I fuck her, the louder she gets, spurring me on. I drive my cock into her slick pussy, palming her breasts as she arches her back off the bed, crying my name. "Keep saying it, babe. Keep telling me what you want."

"Hard, Duke." She gasps as my hips bruise her. "Yes."

Cam tips her head to the side, her neck exposed on such a beautiful angle as she presses into the bed. I slide my hand from her chest over her collarbone, and rest it at her throat to test the waters.

Her pussy clamps on my cock, holding me captive as I flex my fingers a little tighter.

"God, yes," she groans, grinding herself into me. "Do that."

I grip her neck tight, using my hold on her to drive her harder down onto me on the upstroke. Her mouth forms a fuckable "O" as she takes a hold of her tits and pinches her nipples, the sexiest moans wrapping me in a lust-filled haze as I bring the woman to orgasm.

She screams out a string of barely comprehendible expletives as her body crunches in on itself, her muscles tight, choking the hell out of my dick as I increase my pace to the point where I feel like a seventeen-year-old kid busting a nut on his first fuck all over again. She's. That. Good.

"Fuck, Cam." I grit my teeth and jerk my hips, spilling my release into the sweetest woman I've ever met.

So sweet that as much as I feel our connection just now was the only natural way to proceed with what we have, I still can't see how we would ever work.

The devil may have once been an angel, but there's no room for Cam's pure innocence in the circle of hell I'm confined to.

No room at all.

TWENTY-FOUR

CAMMIE

"I can't believe you convinced me to do this. I feel as though I should have a different car, be wearing a wig or something." I glance around the streets as we wait to turn left, but nobody seems to pay any mind to my distinctive BMW.

"Relax," Duke says with a laugh. "You're so on edge all the time. What are your employers going to do if they find out you're not actually sick? You're entitled to use those days however you like, you know."

"I know." I sigh and shift the gears as we head toward the first stop on my fly-by tour of Burbank. "I don't like letting people down, is all. I feel like I'm being dishonest." I glance across at him as he reclines in the passenger seat. "This is paramount to shoplifting for me, you realise?"

"Chill, woman." He rolls his head my way, gracing me with a wide smile.

To think that he would only give me a slight smirk at the start, and yet he hid that gorgeous smile all along. Makes me feel even more special that I get to receive one.

"What's the plan, Stan?" Duke asks, straightening up in his seat as we turn into the public parking area next to the riverbank. "What are we going to do here?"

"Go for a walk." I bring the car to a stop under the overhanging branches of an oak and switch it off. "It's not far. Like, literally just to the riverbank."

He seems satisfied with the idea, and gets out. I snag a bottle of water from my bag before locking the car, and then pocket the keys. Duke stands a little distance away from the car, hands in his pockets as he stares over his head at the branches of the tree.

"What are you doing?"

He breaks from his trance and reaches for my hand. "Something I used to do with Piata when we were bored on patrol."

"Piata?"

He swallows, his jaw flexing as he stares ahead. "He was my best mate. We trained together, ended up in the same unit."

"Was," I echo.

He doesn't say any more about the guy, but I get the distinct feeling Piata was one of the casualties in the attack that maimed Duke.

"Anyway," he says, sucking in a deep breath as we head for the riverbank. "Because the sky was more often than not bluer than blue, we couldn't fuck around making shapes in the clouds. So we'd make shapes between the leaves of the trees. Same principle."

"You must have been bored to do that," I say.

"Insanely so. There's sweet fuck-all to look at in the more remote parts. We could travel for hours without seeing another person. It was eerie to begin with, like driving through a ghost town." He jerks his chin at the river as we come to a stop where the gravelled car park runs out. "What's special about this place?"

"Nothing really. It's just pretty here. Peaceful." I give his hand a squeeze, making him look down at me. "I thought you might appreciate the quiet."

The smile that spreads across his lips and stays there is nothing short of heart-warming.

I end up taking Duke for a walk along the riverbank, pointing out where my friends and I would come as kids in school to swim in the summer months. He appreciates everything I tell him, listening intently as I recount happier times. Times when I was young and had the whole world at my feet, when I wasn't so shaped by the choices I eventually made.

When I was simply me and not my mistakes.

The day disappears in the blink of an eye, our travels taking us back to Donna's café. His company makes me relaxed enough to not care what anyone thinks if they see me on my day off. Like he told me, I'm entitled to them, so why not enjoy the day? We grab a bite to eat and take it with us, ending the tour of my home town at the lookout near the summit of the mountain everybody in Burbank has conquered at least once. The trek is like a rite of passage for anyone who grew up around here, to have made it to the top without passing out. Four hundred and seventy metres, damn near straight up. They don't have ropes on the track for no reason.

Which is why today we drove to the top—took the easy option.

"I forgot how amazing the view is from up here." I

lean back against the windscreen, our afternoon snack laid out between us on the hood of my car as we kick back and enjoy the sight.

Duke stretches out, folding his arms behind his head to give me the best view of his incredible physique. "When was the last time you came and parked up here?"

"Gosh, not since I had Taylah." I'd park at the base and walk the track every couple of months to keep my fitness in check, challenge myself.

But motherhood has that sneaky way of absorbing all your free time without you even thinking about it, and before I realised exactly how little I got for myself, I'd gained fifteen kilograms and consigned myself to a life of stretchy waistbands and comfortable footwear.

Taylah was my only concern, and as long as she was happy, I was happy, and in turn, Jared was happy. At least, I thought he was. I sometimes wonder, with how quickly our relationship broke down, if perhaps he wasn't. Was Taylah's death simply a catalyst for something that already lurked beneath the pretty exterior of our relationship?

"We should do the track before you go," I say, rolling awkwardly to my side so I can face Duke.

He picks at the sausage roll laid out on the paper bag between us, tipping his head to the side. "I guess we could do it on the weekend."

"Sunday," I confirm. "Because Saturday I'm in the theatre all day."

"Deal."

A while passes where neither of us say a thing, too busy picking at our food and staring out at the patchwork of green that covers the flat farmland beyond. Yet I don't feel uncomfortable in our silence. With most people, the lack of conversation gets to me, niggles at my subconscious until I feel panicked into saying something, picking up where the dialogue left off in case the other person is bored by my presence. But with Duke, I feel as though he doesn't expect anything of me. As though the sheer fact we're here together, sharing this amazing view, is enough.

Duke scrunches up the rubbish and twists to his side, reaching around the car to toss the bag in the open passenger's window with a flick of his wrist. I lick my fingers, eyeing his body as he elongates himself. The guy is seriously smoking hot, and I have to bite down on my finger to remind myself that this isn't some fatigue-induced dream.

"Satisfied?" he asks as he rolls onto his back, his head turned my way.

So much. "Feeling good. Thanks."

He extends his closest arm to me, gesturing for me to scoot closer. I slide across the warm metal and tuck myself against his side, resting my head on his bicep. He hums, a melodic sound from deep in his chest, and closes his eyes. "This is nice."

I close my eyes also, inhaling the woody scent of the forest around us mixed with Duke's musky cologne. If perfection could be defined as a moment, a coming together of the senses, this would be it: Duke's smell, the warmth of the dying afternoon sun on my back, his heartbeat beneath my hand, and the sound of the birds as they move through the trees. It's perfect harmony, inside and out.

I relish the peace it brings me, loving the way we don't need to speak to enjoy each other's company. I let my eyes slip closed and tuck into Duke a little tighter as I allow myself to relax completely. Before long I'm fighting the pull of sleep, sated and warm against his side.

"What time do you have to be at the theatre?" Duke asks quietly, his eyes still closed.

I prop myself up on one elbow and look at his gorgeous face as he relaxes in the sun. "Half five." His lashes are dark, his cheekbones strong. He has a classically masculine appearance that adds to his intensity when he watches me with those rich brown eyes of his.

I've never liked being the centre of attention all that much, but I find that as I stare at Duke, wishing he'd open his eyes and look at me, that that gaze of his is what I appreciate the most. The way he looks at me as though I'm the sole focus of his attention, the centre of his world—while he's here in Burbank, at least. Knowing he's leaving, that the feeling won't last? It hurts. Still, I choose not to ruin the now with the what-ifs of the future.

I lean in and place a kiss to his cheek, adding another to his lips. He comes to life as he reciprocates, his lips teasing mine with quick, short sweeps. I pull back to find his eyes open, that chest-warming gaze fixed squarely on me. "You're so fucking beautiful, you know that?"

"As long as you think so, what does it matter if I know it or not?" I'm sceptical, sure he's wrapped up in a bubble of lust that won't last. But hey, I'm not going to stop him if he chooses to see only the best parts of me for now.

Duke reaches up, tucking my hair behind my ear. His fingers linger on the side of my neck, the very tips dancing a line between my earlobe and collarbone. It's soft, sweet, and so damn sensual.

"Thank you," I whisper. "For making me take the day off. I didn't realise how much I've missed out on around here until you made me stop to look at it all again." I drop to my shoulder, tucking in tight to his side again.

"You notice a lot when you pause long enough for everything to stop spinning."

"That you do." Like how I've kept myself shut off from love, thinking I could never deserve to feel that kind of tender connection again.

Jared was the one to walk, but I handed him my heart to take with him. If he didn't want it, neither did I. But at the time, I was heartbroken, and I couldn't see how I'd ever have need for it again.

Not until now.

"We better get moving if we're going to cook you something better than pancakes for dinner again." Duke silently chuckles under my touch.

"Don't dis the fare, man," I tease. "Those pancakes sustained me for most of my twenties."

He shifts, jostling the arm underneath me until he lies on his side, propped up on one elbow. "How old are you, Cam? That's one thing we've never discussed."

"How old do you think I am?" I love this game …

He traces my cheekbones with his thumb, his eyes roving over my face. "You seem like an old soul, so I'm going to guess … mid-twenties."

He can stay. "Thirty, as of two months ago."

"Huh." His eyebrows shoot up. "Although, seeing how your mum's aged, I should have known you'd be older than you appear." He grins. "Your turn. What about me, smartarse?"

I twist my lips to the side. "Hmm …" He has lines around his eyes, and his skin is tanned, as though he sees a lot of sun. But how much of that came from serving overseas in a dry and arid climate? "Mid-thirties?"

He slams a hand to his chest, hissing air in between his teeth. "She slays me."

"You dork," I say on a laugh. "Tell me then."

"Close. Thirty-two."

"What's the big deal?" I tease. "Not as though I said you were forty or anything."

"Would it matter if I was?" He cocks an eyebrow, walking his fingers from my bellybutton up between my breasts to tap me on the chin.

"No. Not at all." I smirk. "You'd make a sexy sugar daddy, I reckon."

The chuckle that rumbles from deep in his chest warms me. It's the most natural, most beautiful sound.

"I don't know how I feel about you calling me 'daddy', babe. Not really my thing."

"Oh yeah?" I wriggle my shoulders back into the hood of the car, making my tits pop. "What is?"

His gaze drops to my chest. *Bingo.* "That's an intimate conversation you've started, Cam."

I run my hands up his chest, squeezing the muscles in his shoulders. "I do believe we were relatively intimate last night, Duke, so surely it doesn't matter."

His lips tilt up in that grin I fell so hard for the first day we met, as he looks at me with hooded eyes. "I guess not."

"Then tell me," I dare him. "What's your thing, soldier?"

"The connection." His palm skates a lazy path around my neck. "Getting lost in the moment, in the person."

Damn, it's hot out here.

"Doesn't matter how the act is done," he tells me in a low, husky tone. "As long as I forget where I am, time, everything—*that's* what makes sex good."

Why the fuck did I start this conversation out in the open? *Holy shit.* I swallow, fighting as my throat sticks. The way he looks at me right now, as though he could devour me ... *damn.*

"Did you?" I murmur. "Last night?"

"Feel that connection?" he asks as he dips his head to leave hot kisses on my neck.

I arch my back, my eyes closed as he palms my side. "Yeah."

Duke's thumb slides along the ridge of my underwire, slow, precise, *torturous.* "What do you think, Cam?"

"Yes," I barely manage to breathe out. "Yes, you did." His bottom lip drags a line from the base of my throat to the point of my chin. "*We* did."

"Damn straight." He takes my mouth with his, a hungry, dominant kiss that tells me I'm all his. *If only it was enough to make him stay.*

"As much as I'd love to repeat last night," he murmurs, "I've got more respect for you than to do it out here."

I sigh in frustration as he pushes himself off me, lying to the side.

"We should get back before those dark clouds turn nasty," he says, jerking his chin at the now grey and formidable sky. "Get you ready for your show."

Have a cold shower, more like. "Yeah. We should."

I slide off the hood with another sigh, unable to hold back my frustration any longer at how quickly this week is passing us by. If Duke notices, he chooses not to say anything, slipping off the side of the hood without a word. We get in the car, the tension from our snatched kisses still thick in the air as I turn the key in the ignition.

Duke slides down the seat as I make my way onto the road, assuming what I've come to know as his position: one foot propped on the side of the centre console. He rolls his head over to look at me, but I don't glance across, watching at him in my periphery instead. If I look at him and catch that smile one more time, I'm liable to cry. Why do I have to find such a perfect guy when he's got a life elsewhere, when our time together has an expiration date?

I've never been one to complain that things aren't fair, but this right here? It's so fucking unfair I want to stop the car and shout it from the roof.

"Tell me what it is that got you into theatre." Duke nudges my leg with his hand, clearly doing his best to break me from my state of self-loathing.

And as much as I hate to admit it, it kind of works. The simple sound of his voice, the soft way in which he shows me he's genuinely interested in what I have to say—it calms me.

"Mum and Dad," I say. "They met doing a show for their college. He was crew, and she was the leading lady. The sweet irony is, over the years, the roles reversed—Mum ended up backstage, and Dad took to the spotlight. I grew up running under the feet of their drama club, so it was only natural that I got roped in when I was old enough to sling stuff around." I glance across at him, hoping that was enough to satisfy his need to break the silence. For once, this chatty girl just wants to wallow in pitiful silence. I'm going to miss this guy, and if simply thinking about how much that is going to hurt pains me like it does now, then how the hell am I going to feel when he actually drives that rat-shit car away for good?

"It's pretty cool that your whole family is into it." His eyes wrinkle just the slightest bit at the sides, and I know he thinks he's got me lured me into more conversation.

The bastard's right. As morose and crappy as I feel right now, I can't help it. I'm a conversationalist—it's what I do.

"Not quite right. Dad doesn't do it anymore. He gave up about the time they split. Sort of awkward, showing your face in your group of friends when *everyone* knows the reason for the divorce." I chuckle as I prepare for the next bit. "He left with his tail between his legs."

"Why did they split?"

"Affair. There was this woman who came out to our little Podunk town here to fill a vacant spot on the cast. She was from one of the big production houses in town." I pause to take a breath, the basic thought of that woman making my blood boil. "Anyway, I remember her because her perfume always made me gag; I was about seven at the time. Dad got busted helping her with more than a costume change between scenes, if you catch my drift."

"That's pretty shit," he says.

"Yeah." I shrug, flexing my hands on the steering wheel. "But better to be confronted with the issue and deal with it than have him sneaking around for years, right? I mean, as much as it hurt to know, I was always thankful that I knew exactly why Jared left. I would have hated for him to get away with it for years, for him to have the chance to waste my life away like that. At least—even though it's taken me a while to regain myself—I have the chance to move on." *With you.*

Duke says nothing, simply staring at me, his hair all messed up where it'd dragged down the seat in his slump. "I guess. Being overseas would mess with my head sometimes, make me wonder what was gong on back at home, you know?"

"You didn't trust your wife?"

He frowns before looking away. "Yeah, I trusted her. That's why I felt so shit about still wondering, being jealous like that. It wasn't fair on her when she never did a thing to give me reason to worry."

"It must have been hard on her, huh? Having you away for so long?"

"It was hard on both of us." He falls silent, staring at the road ahead for a while before he continues. "Still, that stuff is in the past. I don't want to be thinking about it when I'm here spending the day with you." He reaches across, taking my hand closest to him in his.

"I don't want you to leave," I whisper, afraid that if I don't say it now he'll never truly know how deeply the thought cuts at me.

"I know."

We continue on in silence, Duke seemingly lost in his thoughts as he stares out the side window, and me trapped in a battle between wanting to let go of his hand, wanting to cry if I don't, and wanting to hold on.

The first spots of rain hit the windscreen as I slow for my driveway, a sickness laying root in my gut at the thought that another day is almost at a close. The sickness turns to nausea when we near the house and find a black truck already parked outside.

"Shit." I stop the car, Duke ramrod straight in the passenger seat beside me.

"Is that who I think it is?"

"Jared." I pull the keys out as the man in question steps off the porch.

Duke's out of the car before I can say another word. I scramble to get out, the pace at which Duke strides towards Jared unsettling.

"What are you doing here?" I call out, interjecting before Duke can get a word in edgeways.

Jared eyes Duke from head to toe, and then walks straight past him to meet me halfway as the drizzle turns to rain. "I have a contract for you to sign."

"For Amanda?"

"Terry." The arsehole smirks. If Duke doesn't deck him first, I think I might.

"I told you I wanted Amanda," I remind him in a low, level tone that belies my rage.

"And I thought Terry was a better fit." He thrusts the envelope, no doubt containing the contract, toward me.

I snatch it before it falls to the wet ground and then promptly throw it back at him. "Come back when you have the right one."

Jared opens his mouth to speak, yet stops as Duke steps in between us, his back to me, one hand to Jared's chest. "I think you should leave."

"Get your hands off me." Rain soaks Jared's shirt where Duke presses it, sticking the navy cotton to his hard chest.

I step out of the way as Duke lifts his hands and backs away with a tip of his head. "No problem, mate. But if I hear about you making Cam upset again, my hands on you is going to be the least of your worries."

"Are you threatening me?" Jared crumples his face up, making out he can't believe what he just heard. He looks to me, rain dripping off his nose as he thumbs at Duke. "Did he threaten me just then, Cam?"

"I believe he did." I turn the corners of my mouth down, lifting my eyebrows as though surprised.

The rain intensifies, running in rivers down my face, over my arms. Yet I don't care. It's relief, a reminder that I'm alive. I'm doing okay. I'm strong enough to stand my ground with this and not let Jared bully me into doing what he wants like he has during the past three years.

"I can't believe this shit." Jared bends down, snatching up the sodden envelope. "First you kill our kid, and now you refuse to move out of the house like some goddamn squatter."

Kill our kid ... "What did you say?"

Duke lunges forward, shoving a hand into Jared's shoulder. "Get in your fucking truck and go."

I don't even have time to say anything as Jared draws his free arm back and throws a wayward punch at Duke. My heart leaps into my throat as Duke dodges and then promptly takes a hold of Jared's arm, twisting it behind him. The men tussle, hair wet in their faces as Jared tries to regain the upper hand—which should be easy, given he's taller—yet he fails. A height advantage is nothing compared to a trained fighter. Duke tangles his foot in Jared's, effectively immobilising him unless my ex fancies a date with the driveway.

"Calm your shit, man," Duke warns. "This doesn't need to get out of hand."

"You'll be hearing from my lawyer," Jared bellows, breaking free with a violent twist of his shoulders. He throws the envelope in the open door of his truck and turns back to face us both. "If these are the kinds of people you welcome into our home, Cam, then I may as well let your mum know she should plan your funeral now." He throws a hate-filled glare at Duke. "Because with a violent arsehole like him, you're bound to end up raped and murdered."

Duke cracks up laughing, tossing his head back, his thumbs hooked in his jeans as Jared gets in the truck and slams the door. It unsettles my ex, which I couldn't love more. Yet what intrigues me is that he doesn't even appear to be doing it for show—Duke's genuinely amused by Jared's attitude.

The truck kicks stones up toward the house, spattering them over the veranda, yet they don't appear to make a sound thanks to the deluge we're now caught in.

"He come here to do that often?" Duke asks as we head the house.

"I've seen him more in the last month than I have in the last year." I shake my dripping hair off my face, wiping it out of the way with my hands.

Duke takes one look at me and chuckles. "Oh, Cam."

"What?" I fish through my bag for where I tossed the keys when I went after the men.

"You've got makeup from your lashes down to your jaw."

I roll my eyes at him before I slot the key in the door. "I can imagine." My gaze returns to him as I twist and open. "You're not all that put together yourself, you know."

His light grey T-shirt is drenched, sticking to the planes of his muscles, his hair dripping water onto his face that runs in slow lines down to the sharp edge of his jaw before falling to the deck.

"We going inside?" he asks quietly, drawing my attention to the fact I stand in the open doorway with my fingers still wrapped around the handle.

"Oh, shit. I mean, yeah. Of course."

My favourite smirk returns as I step into the entrance and drop my bag. Duke shuts the door behind us as I hop around on one foot, trying to peel my sodden boots off. I manage to wrestle them into submission and drop the shoes on the floor before peeling my cardigan off as well. Silence echoes between us as I let the clothing hit the floor with a wet thwack.

"How long have you got before you need to go out again?"

"About an hour." I turn to face Duke. "Why—"

Oh, my.

He's stripped off his wet shirt, standing in my entrance in only his soaked jeans with his belt and the button of his jeans undone.

"I thought I should take them off so I didn't make your carpet wet with the bottoms on the way to the laundry." He gestures at the dark legs of his jeans, and then my hallway rug.

"Yeah." I swallow, glancing down at the pools my leggings make on the floor. "I should probably do the same."

Duke's wet jeans swish across the hardwood floor as he closes the space between us in three long strides, his hands rising to my hips to lift me off the floor and carry me with him until my back finds the wall.

I hit the plaster with enough force to knock the air from my lungs, my chest burning given I don't get a chance to draw another breath before Duke's mouth is on mine.

Holding me in place with his hips, he brings both hands to my face, pushing my wet hair out of the way as he tilts his head and deepens our kiss. I allow his to consume me, wanting to be as much a part of him as he already is of me. He's been inside my head since he first admitted he needed help on the roadside, so it's only fair that I get a chance to infect him also.

Maybe then he'll stay? Maybe if he gets enough of me, feels the way I need him here in order to keep treading water and being able to breathe, he'll come back?

God, I hope so. Because with how deeply I'm falling in love with this man, I can only imagine the separation will tear me apart when he takes a chunk of who I am with him.

"You deserve so much more," he mutters, his eyes closed as he presses his forehead to mine, his hands still braced against the sides of my face. "You deserve love."

"I deserve yours," I whisper, lifting my chin to kiss his nose.

Duke drops me to the floor, my feet only just getting under me in time to take my weight as he hooks both hands in my leggings and shoves downward, hard. I step out of the wet fabric, helping him as he yanks them off in what can only be described as murderous frustration.

He pauses to look at my thong, and frowns. "No time."

I gasp, my arms wrapping around his shoulders on instinct as he hitches me up his body again, using one of the hands braced under my arse to hook the thin strip of fabric over my pussy aside. I reach between us, my heartbeat thundering like a marching band as I wrestle his boxers out of the way and free his hard length.

He enters me in one short, rough thrust, shunting me up the wall with determination as he drives into me over and over.

I close my eyes and moan at how full, how complete he makes me feel. His lips are hot on my neck, his tongue hotter still as he tastes the water that runs across my flesh. Duke's forearms cage me in, pressed flat against the wall on either side of my head, and I couldn't love that more. I feel wrapped up in him, lost in him ... *as though I'm his.*

"So ... fucking ... beautiful," he grinds out between thrusts hard enough to make the bruises that linger from last night ache. All I can do is hold on as this man destroys me in the most beautiful of ways. Hold on to my heart for fear I'll lose it again to another man who'll leave me when I need him most.

Duke's legs buckle as he jerks his release, our bodies entwined as we fall to the floor. I'm so close, and he must know it, as he shuffles back, taking me with him so he can keep going missionary style on the wet timber.

The sight of this man holding me to him, the intensity in his eyes as he focuses on my pleasure—it doesn't take long before I follow him over that cliff, diving into the deep and sinking in his embrace. Realising that as much as this man has managed to bring my life, my love back into the light, he's also the very thing that's going to finally kill me.

TWENTY-FIVE

DUKE

"Thanks again for the lift." I put my hand on the door, ready to get out when Cammie's mum stops me in my tracks.

"What happens now, Duke?"

Fuck. I called her knowing that A) Cammie would flip when she heard the HQ was ready early, and B) that if I waited until Cam was home to give me a lift into town, I wouldn't get here before Archie did the school run.

"How do you mean, Clara?"

She twists in her seat to face me better. "I may be getting old, but I'm no fool. I know what it looks like when two people have strong feelings for one another."

She saw us last night at the show, came and sat next to me for the second act, beside Cammie's platform as she did her thing on the spotlight.

"I don't know," I say with a sigh, ceding that this conversation won't be over soon and relaxing back into the seat. "I thought I could give us a chance, see where it leads, but we can't deny the crux of it all."

"That you won't stick around," Clara says with a sigh. Her eyes are hard, her expression impassive, yet

I've never felt more schooled in my life.

"That I don't live here," I correct. "My life is somewhere else."

"She's been through a lot, my daughter," she says in her we're-no-longer-friends, I'm-her-mother tone. "I thought I could trust that you'd be honourable enough to only take things in this direction if you had good intentions for her."

"I do have good intentions," I snap. "And that's why I think it's best I cool things off, give her distance to make up her own mind."

"Break her heart, more like," Clara mumbles.

I shove the door open, stepping out into the overcast day before turning and popping my head down to Clara's level. "If she let herself get that attached while knowing I was leaving, then Cam's gone and broken her own heart."

It's a low blow, but there it is—the truth, laid out bare.

I shut the door and storm off toward the workshop, pissed not only at her mother for trying to emotionally blackmail me into changing my whole fucking life for a woman that I met less than a week ago, but also at myself for wanting to.

If there are two things I can't deny about Cam, it's that women like her aren't a dime a dozen, and the fact that she makes my heart race, my chest tight whenever she's near ... I feel something more than a passing interest.

"Duke," Archie calls as I enter the work bay. "Good to see you."

Although I get the impression it's not because he

likes me, more as if he's glad it means he gets rid of the HQ *and* me.

"Did it behave on the test drive?" I walk around the vehicle, impressed he's gone so far as to give it a quick wash.

"Like a dream." He steps over to a pegboard and removes the keys. "Came in on budget, more or less. Extra thirty-five over, but I'll let it pass."

"Nah, mate. I'll square you up." I take the offered keys.

"I owe Cammie for all the things she buys the kids when she babysits, anyway." He drills his gaze into mine. "Besides, I'm sure you're eager to get on your way." I get the clear message this conversation is about more than just a car and a mechanical bill. Seems like everyone in this town has my number.

"Thanks, I guess."

He nods, folding his arms over his chest. "Looks like you've got no reason to stick around anymore; time to go home."

"Apparently." I move the keys between my hands, unsure if the guy plans to take me down or simply let me go with a few underhanded comments.

"Heard what you did to Jared."

Fuck it. "That so?" I tuck my bottom lip up and frown. "News travels fast, then."

"Small town, *mate.*" He grimaces on the last word. "Better make sure you don't come across her cousin again on your way out."

Nope—totally not feeling ganged up on I open the door to the HQ, stepping a leg inside as I brace myself with a hand on the roof. "We all done here, then?"

Archie nods, stepping back. "Safe travels, Duke."

I drop into the seat and close the door on his bullshit, starting the V8 with a roar. He watches me go, unmoving in my rear-view as I pull out of the workshop and take to the road.

"Fuck it!" I slam the heel of my hand into the steering wheel.

How did I let things get so complicated? All I had to do was stay a few days in some stranger's house and be done with it. Could have kept my dick to myself and thought things through with the *useful* brain in my head, but no, I had to go and jump in feet first.

I don't know what's worse—the fact I did this to Cam, or the look she'll no doubt give me when I break the news that it's time for me to go. *Although the car in the driveway should do a good job of that.*

My thoughts play on repeat the whole drive back to her place, and yet, after fifteen minutes of the same loop, I'm no better off than I was when I left the workshop.

Taking a seat in the sun on the front porch, I pull my phone out and dial Cody. He'll be glad that the car's fixed. At least I can keep *one* person happy. Shit.

"Hey, bro," he greets as he picks up the call.

"Slow day at work then, if you're answering your phone. Thought I'd have to leave you a voicemail."

"Boss is away," he says with nothing short of mischief in his voice. "IT took the blocks off the net, too, so we're all fucking around."

The work ethic of this one ... honestly. "Car's running."

"Sweet. I'll start paying you back next month."

"Like fuck, you little turd. You'll transfer the first hundred the minute I get—"

"Relax," he says, laughing. "I was winding you up, man. Shit. What's crawled up your arse?"

Curvy little woman by the name of Cam, that's what.

"Nothing. Ask Mum if she wants me to pick anything up from town on my way home."

"Yeah, I'll get her to message you. When you leaving?"

"Tomorrow." My gaze falls on the scuffmarks in the gravel where I restrained Jared last night. *Hopefully Cam will be okay.*

"Sweet. See you then, bro."

"Yeah. Catch you then." I end the call and crush the phone in my hand, the pain of the case as it digs into my palm a welcome anchor in what's been my first anxious moment in days.

She's a grown woman—she can hold her own.

But she shouldn't have to. That's just it. A woman like her deserves to have a strong man by her side to defend her when jackasses like her ex show up. Just because a woman can fight her own battles doesn't mean she should have to. Especially when she's the kind of woman who merits the sort of love that precedes sacrifice.

I spend the next hour and a bit before Cammie's due home taking a shower and packing the HQ with my things—not that there's much. I leave my new phone charger out to unplug and take with me when I go.

When I go.

I'm still stuck on that thought when the nose of Cam's car comes into view down the driveway. I stay where I'm seated, back on the porch, wanting to see her reaction when she spots the HQ.

It's not pretty.

Her car switches off, parked so that I can't see her inside it, but the fact she doesn't get out straight away is unsettling. A solid ten minutes pass before she opens the door and storms across the yard, straight past me and into the house.

Shit.

Guess I should go find out how bad it is, then.

"Cam?" I call as I shut the front door behind me. "Can we talk?"

She flies out of her bedroom at the far end of the hall, on the warpath. "When are you leaving?"

"Tomorrow." I tuck my hands in my pockets for fear if I leave them free, I might end up with her against the wall again.

"Fuck you." She screws her face up, shaking her head at me ... and then storms back into her room, slamming the door behind her.

Okay then ...

Went well, considering.

I take my time walking up the hall to her bedroom, and stop outside the closed door. I can't pick up any sounds from beyond it. I suppose that's a good thing because it means she can't be crying.

I rap my knuckles on her door. "Cam?"

"Go away!"

Not yet. I open the door to find her cross-legged on her bed, her face a storm. "I get that you're angry—"

"I'm hurt."

And then the tears begin.

"I'm hurt because you're fucking leaving still," she whines, fat tears leaking over her face. "And I'm mostly pissed off because I knew you would, but I'm still surprised by it. Urgh!" She hurls a pillow across the room, its soft landing against the wall not seeming to satisfy her when she picks up her phone and prepares to throw that, too.

"Put it down." I lunge and grab her wrist, forcing her to drop the damn thing before she has to fork out a grand to replace it.

"Why?" she cries, her face utter betrayal.

"Am I going?" I ask, knowing she's not asking why I told her to put the phone down. "You know why, babe. I've got counselling, a job to sort out ..."

"No." She shakes her head vehemently, ripping her arm from my hold. "Why am I not enough?"

Crap. She *is* enough. It's *me* who isn't all he's cracked up to be. "You're everything," I tell her. "Too much."

Her nostrils flare, the light catching her bullring as it moves. "Too much," she murmurs angrily. "That's bullshit, Duke." Her small hands shunt me hard in the chest, yet I don't move. I sit on the bed with her instead. The more she pushes me away, the closer I want to be.

"The space to breathe will do you good."

She frowns, leaning in close to utter with so much hate it makes me hurt, "I'll drown."

Fuck—she will. But as much as it pains me to let her go, she needs to learn to swim on her own.

I rise from the bed, taking two steps toward the door. "Maybe I should just go now. It might be easier."

She doesn't answer me, turning her head to stare at the darkening sky outside.

It's the loudest silence.
The hardest truth.

TWENTY-SIX

CAMMIE

He left me that night. Pushed my sofas back to how they used to be and walked out the door. I'm still sinking.

"Spot two." Mary's terse call breaks me from my daze.

Shoot. The light's nowhere near my frustrated leading lady.

"Sorry."

"Come see me after. LX35, ready ... and go."

The lights change, the scene picking up pace as my gut sinks. I've been in a funk since Duke went home. I realised too late that I don't even know his number to call—never thinking to get it since I could always reach him at the house—and now I don't have the kahunas to ask Archie what it is. He literally left my life without a trace, other than an overgrown lawn that still looks pretty in stripes.

I buckle down and manage to get through the rest of the Saturday night show without losing focus again, keeping my arm too close to the light in places so that the burn keeps me alert.

The crowd filters out as Susie crosses over from her platform, the frown on her face telling me she's concerned before she even opens her mouth. "What's going on, love?"

"Nothing." I flick my hair out of the way, stashing my half-empty water bottle in my bag, knowing when I get home that I'll stack it with the others just so I feel like Duke is still around.

"You can't bullshit a bullshit artist." She gives me a tight-lipped smile.

I slump down on the edge of my platform, my bag slung between my legs. "That guy who stayed with me?"

"Duke?"

"You remember his name?" I frown. She didn't even talk to him when he came the other night.

"I think everyone in town knows his name," she deadpans. "Nobody's seen you that happy in years."

Urgh. "He left."

"Well, no duh." She screws her top lip up. "He had to take the car home, right?"

I narrow my gaze on her. "Just how much *did* everyone talk about us?"

Susie rubs a nervous hand over the back of her neck. "A little."

"Great." I push to my feet abruptly enough that she takes a hasty step backward. "I better go see Mary."

I get my arse handed to me on a platter. Mary's the type that takes no shit, and if you've got issues outside the theatre she doesn't care, which suits me fine. I need somebody to slap me back into line. I don't want to be babied over a pathetic broken heart. I shouldn't be letting Duke's departure hurt me this much—he was only here for six days.

And yet it felt like a lifetime.

I manage to get as far as my car before my carefully stacked tower of confidence slips and topples. A part of me is thankful for the lack of streetlights near the parking lot as I rest my head on the steering wheel and burst into tears, but the remainder of me is torn apart as I sit in the very thing that reminds me of Duke the most: the darkness.

"Get it together, Cam," I whisper to myself. I can't let myself fall to pieces—not yet, anyway. I have to stay strong considering Jared is coming over with the new contract tomorrow. It seems Duke did one good thing before he left: he scared my ex enough to ensure I have the agent I want for the sale.

Ridiculous. I would have signed with Terry if it meant keeping Duke here longer. If only I had one more day.

I damn near jump out of my skin as a solid knock sounds on my window. "Holy, shit!" Clicking the key around one, I drop the window and frown at Bevan. "I almost died of a heart attack."

"Better than dying because you wallowed in your heart*ache,*" he counters.

"Touché." I look over his shoulder at Susie standing a little way back, having a smoke. "What do you two want?"

"You." Bevan reaches out and opens my door. "We're heading to the pub. I'd ask if you want to come, but it's not up for negotiation."

"I'm not dressed for it," I protest weakly, touched that they want to include me.

"Shut up," Susie teases, stamping her smoke out. "It's Burbank. You'd fit right in wearing stubbies and gumboots."

"I said to leave you alone," Bevan explains, "but Susie here was adamant we can't stand by and watch you self-destruct." He rubs a hand over his stubbled jaw. "I realise we're just theatre buddies and all that, but you know—"

"We thought you might like company," Susie finishes for him.

I do—not theirs, is all. "Fine. A drink can't hurt."

"Fine," Bevan echoes, putting my window up. "We're getting an Uber." He reaches in and snags my keys. "Grab your bag, princess."

I spend the ride to the pub wondering how in the hell I was so blind that I didn't notice a burgeoning romance between these two. *Oh, that's right—I had a moody soldier keeping me distracted.* Susie does her best to fend Bevan off, probably aware how the sight of them cosying up might affect me, but I can see it. They're smitten with each other. I want to punch them each in the face, and then dance on their happiness.

The local rugby team pour in fresh on the heels of another victory as I nurse my vodka at the bar. Sweat and testosterone envelops me as the burly guys crowd into the only available spots to order their drinks.

Susie squeezes in between what appears to be a prop and me. "Plenty of talent for you tonight."

Talent, aka fuckable men.

"I'm not interested." Not when the thought of getting naked with anyone but Duke makes me feel physically ill. *So ruined.*

"Come on." She nudges me as Bevan hands her a new drink. "Have a dance at least. If I wanted you to sit around feeling sorry for yourself, I would have let you go home."

One look at her sorrowful face and I know I should. They've done me good, making sure I come out tonight. The least I can do is *try* to have fun.

The troublesome duo spends the next two hours plying me with drinks until I'm literally one of the last left on the small dance floor, shaking my arse to some song I've never heard before. It's not pretty, but thanks to the numbing effects of the vodka sloshing around in my empty stomach, I don't care.

I'm still sober enough, though, that the attention my uncoordinated dancing gets doesn't go unnoticed.

"You need to slow down," Mr Tall-and-Jacked-Rugby-Player says as he slides in behind me, his hands to my hips.

I move out of his reach, not wanting him to touch me, but not minding the distraction his conversation provides. "I'm fine," I slur, slicing my hand through the air.

He chuckles, steadying me on my feet. The guy's quite handsome: blond hair, chiselled jaw, thick neck. In another time, maybe ... "How about you sit down and I'll get you a water?"

I shrug. Sitting isn't a bad idea; my feet hurt. "Okay."

I look around for Susie and Bevan as he steers me toward an empty table tucked around the side of the bar, but whether it's my blurred vision, or the dim lights in here, I don't know—I can't see them.

My arse hits the seat, and by the time the rugby guy comes back with an iced water, I'm almost asleep with my head on the table.

"Thanks," I murmur, reaching for the glass and managing to avoid spilling it in the nick of time.

"Cammie, right?"

"How do you know?" I point what I hope is an angry finger his way, my head still on the table, but given his smile I'd say I don't quite pull it off.

"You went to school with my big sister."

Of course I did. Wait. Did he say big sister?

"How old are you?" I ask sceptically.

"Twenty-five. Why?"

Pfft. Baby. "No reason."

I manage to get the glass to my lips and sip the tasteless water. Ugh.

"What brings you out tonight?" Rugby Boy asks. "You're not usually here on a Saturday."

"Usually too busy," I answer. *Sitting at home, wallowing in my misery.*

Fuck drunk tears. I swipe at my face, trying to stop the flow.

"You okay?" he asks. "Should we step outside and find you somewhere quiet, more private?"

Because somewhere quieter where the echo of Duke's words will fill my head like angry thunder is *exactly* what I need. "No. I'm fine." I use my sleeve to wipe the last of the tears away. "Do I look okay?" I ask hopefully, aware I probably resemble a road kill racoon about now.

He smirks, handing me a paper napkin. "You might want to go to the ladies to use the mirror."

"Right." God, I'm such a mess.

I push to my feet using the table as ballast, and head in the general direction of the toilets. I only need to correct my wayward path a couple of times, which, given how many vodkas I've consumed tonight, is quite the achievement.

I push through the swing door to find exactly where Susie and Bevan went.

"You realise I can see your reflection in the mirror," I announce. "You really should check you shut the stall door properly."

"Oh my God," Susie exclaims slamming the door shut.

Frantic whispers ensue before she appears, looking rather sheepish, Bevan in tow. "Sorry, Cam."

"It's okay." I wave my hand dismissively at them … and then promptly vomit into a hand basin.

"Oh, shit," Bevan cries, doing the typical male thing by backing away from the mess in such a rush that he collides with the wall.

"Fuck, Cam." Susie, on the other hand, rushes to my side to scoop my hair out of the way. "Time to go home, huh?"

"I don't want to ruin your night," I mumble into the basin as I turn the tap on.

She exchanges a look with Bevan in the mirror and sighs. "It's okay, honey. Your welfare comes first."

"No." I swat a hand at her, hitting her shoulder. "Rugby Boy can take me home later."

"Rugby Boy?" Bevan suddenly finds his balls,

stepping forward into the fray.

"That young thing out there who gave me water to drink."

They exchange another look before Bevan announces, "I'll go talk to him."

"Honestly," I call after him before the door swings shut. "He'll be fine with it."

I have no idea if he will, but just because my love life spent all of six days trying to fly before it crashed from its nest in an angry, wrinkly pink ball doesn't mean Susie and Bevan can't start something beautiful here tonight. Even if it is rather shocking and somewhat unhygienic in a bathroom stall.

Each to their own, I guess.

By the time I've wiped my face clear and chewed a dozen of Susie's mints, Bevan returns looking suitably satisfied.

"Nixon will take her home," he tells Susie. "He's not drinking. On that mega-serious training shiz for the provincial team."

"Nixon?" I ask, double-checking there's no vomit in the ends of my hair.

"Yeah. Jimmy Nixon. That's who you were talking to."

"Oh." *Winning.* "Thanks for checking with him. You two go enjoy yourselves."

I shoo them out the door as two drunk women crash in, doing a double take at Bevan standing in the ladies.

"I'm leaving," he acquiesces, his hands raised.

Susie pushes him out the door, but not before placing a quick kiss to my cheek. "Be careful. And message me if it turns ugly; I'll come right back."

"Go," I repeat, waving them goodbye as the pair disappear up the hallway back to the bar.

I manage to make it back to the table in a singular straight line, but Jimmy's not there. *Whatever.* I take a seat anyway, knocking back half the glass of water.

"Hey, you're back."

I turn my head to my left to find my chivalrous rugby boy standing with a huge grin on his face.

I plaster a matching, yet fake, one on mine to say, "I sure am," with as much gusto as possible.

Yep, I'm back. Because if not here, then where? Not as though I have anything to go home to anymore.

Or anyone.

TWENTY-SEVEN

DUKE

"THESE ARE GREAT." THE GOVERNMENT-APPOINTed therapist flicks through the pages of the journals I've kept these past weeks.

It's been twenty-four days since I left Cammie in Burbank, and the only way I've coped through the dark hours is by throwing myself into the journaling she suggested I do.

"I have a lot of time on my hands," I say simply, leaving out the part where I'm still living with my mother at thirty-two years old because I can't find a job, journaling in the dark, with a torch by my side.

One step at a time.

"Well, I can tell from the few words I've read that you really pour your heart into them, Duke." Dr Dench sets the books aside, placing her hands one atop the other on her sensible suit skirt. "How about we start with a little about you. If I were to ask you to describe yourself in three words, what would you say to me?"

She gives me her undivided attention, which I don't like. I've only tolerated that from one person, and she's not here right now.

"I don't know."

"Take a moment to think about it, and then give me the first words that spring to mind."

Selfish. Stubborn. Dead.

"Strong, I guess."

"Good." She sits patiently, watching me as though waiting for more.

"Honest, and lo—" I stop myself before I say the lie: loyal. "Um, resilient."

"Good." Her eyes narrow in on me, yet her expression manages to stay soft. "What else can you share with me, Duke?"

"I'm not sure what you're expecting." I shift around on the seat, the vinyl tacky under my hot legs. I'm an anxious mess.

"We might be new to each other," she says carefully, "but I've been at this game for a while, and I can see when one of my clients has something on their mind."

She doesn't say it outright, but I can tell she's not going to let us carry on until we've addressed this particular issue. I could bullshit, give her something inconsequential, but I'm guessing she'd see right through that, too.

"It's in the journals," I say, pointing to the pile. "Reading that will probably be better than trying to get me to voice it."

"Okay," she says, resting a hand on the stack. "How about we leave our session here today. We've managed to establish ourselves, get the introductions out of the way." Her fingers tap the top journal. "I'll have a read of these tonight, and we can pick up where we left off in a couple of days when I'm scheduled to see you again."

"Sure." I rise when she does, taking her offered hand and shaking it firmly in mine.

"As always, if you feel you need to talk to someone you can ring through to our offices any time; there's an option to divert to the helpline after hours."

"I'll keep that in mind."

She lets my hand go, standing with her hands folded before her as I take my leave. The receptionist gives me a shy smile as I pass by—her flirting when I arrived didn't escape my notice. Truth is, I'm just not interested. In anything. Especially life now that I'm back in the same old rut.

Coming home was a good thing in that I've spent time with Mum like I said I would. I treated that woman like utter and complete crap for the first year or so after I returned. Every ounce of resentment and injustice I felt I took out on her, and I never once thanked her for what she did for me.

For what she sacrificed.

My mother took a second job to ensure that I didn't have to, making sure I was available to attend every physical therapy session I could to get me to the point I'm at today: where I can walk without a limp.

My leg is a scarred mess, and if Cam noticed it when she saw me naked, she chose not to say a thing.

Yet another tiny detail I realised I appreciated while journaling my thoughts about her. At first, the differences between us drove me nuts, but as I filled the pages with my scrawled words, I realised those quirks were part of what I loved about her. I love the woman for not only her qualities but also her faults. I love all of her.

All I can hope is that this space gives her time to heal, to remember who she was before her life got torn apart. I need Cam to remember how to swim.

How to survive.

How to love herself.

TWENTY-EIGHT

APRIL DENCH SAT DOWN IN HER OVERSIZED armchair with the man's journals in her hand. She pulled the cashmere blanket over her legs and made a space for her cat, Sunny, to fit in beside her.

Lance Corporal Harwood was experiencing a definite case of denial if ever she'd seen one. All army men started out the same: stubborn and staunch. But there was something different about Duke. He knew his faults, and yet he *still* tried to deny their existence.

She shuffled the pile, moving the black bound book to the top. His eye had tracked to it repeatedly, so logic indicated she should start there. She drew a deep breath and opened to the first page. Intricate designs were scrawled over the paper in no particular image or shape, more like somebody was doodling while they tried to work through a thought. She flicked to the next page—blank—and then the third.

With her heart in her throat, she tracked over the inked words, absorbing the information laid out before her in such vivid detail that she felt as though she were there with him, serving right alongside. This man, this soldier ... she'd never encountered such a tortured soul.

But what made her set the book down in her lap and take a moment to breathe was the way he spoke of *her.* Whoever this woman was, this "Cammie" or "Cam" as he sometimes referred to her, she was instrumental to the beginning of his healing; a blind man could see that.

Duke *had* to reconnect with Cam.

April reached for her notepad laid out on the side table, Sunny mewling his protest at being jostled in her haste. She brought the jotter to her lap, laying it out on top of the journal and scratched the simple word at the top: *Cam.*

With her pen in between her lips, she stared at the jotter before setting it aside and continuing with the journal. The hours passed, Sunny shifted to the rug on the floor, and yet April kept going, absorbing, consuming, detailing until the last page had been turned.

Dawn crept on the horizon as she set her jotter aside, the corner of the pages crumpled from her constant flicking back and forth. Words were scrawled so hard in places, the lines repeated on rote as she worked through a train of thought, she'd literally pushed through to the page beyond.

But through it all, through the story of this man's life, she'd found one thing he hadn't. A crucial element to his personality that he had neither named or recognised during her questioning.

Hope.

Duke still possessed hope, still retained the simple ability to look beyond, to plan ahead, and some of his counterparts didn't.

And that, his hope, would be the thing that brought him salvation. She was sure of it.

TWENTY-NINE

CAMMIE

Sunlight dances in patterns across my palm as I lie on the sofa, my arm slung over the side to rest on the floor. I twist my fingers back and forth watching the slivers of gold that morph and merge on my flesh.

"Are you only taking the three boxes to the Salvation Army, love?" Mum flits between the entrance and Taylah's room, finishing what I started.

"At this stage."

It may have taken me four or five attempts, but finally, after changing my mind almost daily about it, I stepped inside her room last week to begin the task of selecting what to keep and what to be donated to children in need.

The agent has a fair offer on the house—not my parents'—and if nothing else, I know for certain that my time here is limited.

Five weeks have passed since Duke left, and I think it's fair to say my last reason to stay here left that day, too. I've let go of the torment over Taylah that kept me shackled to this house as though it were a shrine to my daughter. The only good memories I had left here were those I shared with him. And now he's gone and ruined those, too.

"Mum?"

She pokes her head around the corner. "Yes?"

I can almost smell how eager she is from here. She's been on at me to talk to her for weeks … since Duke left, really. But I've kept her at arm's length, a little mad and harbouring a grudge over the fact it was *her* meddling that got us involved to begin with.

"Can I ask you something?"

"Of course." She adjusts her messy bun as she glides into the room, settling on the floor beside me.

"Do you believe in love at first sight?"

Her hands go to her chest as her eyebrows rise in the middle. "Oh, Cam."

"Is it possible to know in such a short time the truth of how you feel about a person, or do you think that feelings will always change?"

Her hands drop to her lap, and she places one to the side to lean her weight on it. "I believe that yes, people's feelings do change over time, but it's more of an adjustment. You learn to accommodate a person, to live with the things that may have irked you at the start, and likewise, you learn to adjust the things you do that irk them." She pauses, rubbing her lips together. "But … I also believe that the root of what first brought you together never changes. If you love someone, you love them; it's that simple."

"Do you still love Dad, then?"

She shrugs. "I love him, but I'm not *in* love with him. Regardless, the way I feel about him is still different to how you love a friend."

"Hmm."

She picks my hand up, massaging the palm with her thumbs. "What have you been thinking about, love?"

"Everything."

The way I coped in the first two weeks after Duke left can only be described as chaos in motion. The after-show drinks at the pub turned out to be the first of several nights when I ended up so shit-faced I couldn't remember how I got there.

But then the show ended.

And with that went my last reason to keep busy, keep occupied. I crashed hard and spectacularly, breaking down in the middle of the office at work, tears tracking over my face no matter what I did to try and stop them.

Three forced sick days later, and I assured my boss that I could return to work without combusting at the simplest word or sound. I came back swinging, stronger than ever, doing things I had avoided for years.

Like sorting Taylah's room.

But through it all, I've remained empty, devoid of direction as I float under the surface of my black sea, watching the sunshine make patterns on the surface. I've achieved a lot, and yet the victory seems so hollow.

"You know I have his number, Cammie." Mum squeezes my hand, begging me in her silent way to accept it, to try.

"What would I say?"

"That you're a stubborn old mule, and that you miss him."

I snort, closing my eyes. "He made it clear his life

wasn't here with me, Mum. If he thought it could be, he would have come back."

In hindsight, I guess that's why the first weeks were the hardest—I lived in the limbo Duke had spoken of, hoping he would return to sweep me off my feet.

But he didn't.

"Then I don't know what else I can say," Mum tells me as she sets my hand down and stands. "You know the answer, and yet you'd rather suffer than bruise your ego by accepting you both made a mistake in choosing to carry on with separate lives."

"How am I bruising my ego?" I cry. "He left me."

"And you did nothing to change that," she says. "Make a damn phone call, Cam, and be done with it. If he rejects you twice, you can let it go and move on. I'm sick of seeing you miserable over something you could fight to change if you really wanted another chance with him that badly."

She doesn't get it. I might be miles from the shore, but my drifting has distanced me from the shipwreck all the same. If I call him, hear his voice, bring the echoes to life, then I put myself back at the start. If he rejects me again, then I'm forced to hang up and face the fact he lives somewhere else, has a life away from here all over again.

I'm forced to say goodbye a second time, and I don't know if I'm strong enough do that.

"What time does the Salvos shut?" I swing my legs around and sit myself up.

"Four," Mum mumbles, heading back into Taylah's room.

"I'll throw these boxes in the car then and get them

into town."

Because the sooner we get this over with, the sooner Mum goes home. And the sooner my mother leaves, the sooner I can go to bed and lie awake pretending my nightmares aren't my life, and my dreams aren't where I wish to be.

THIRTY

DUKE

"I'VE PUT THE LAST OF THE THINGS THAT WERE IN your wardrobe in the attic for sorting another day, Son." Mum dusts her sleeves off as she stands in the kitchen doorway, bits of insulation clinging to the cotton. "You know, I've enjoyed having you home, even if you have been distracted for the more recent part of it."

"I enjoyed it, too."

She lifts her chin to look me squarely in the eye. "Any idea when you might be back?"

I shake my head. "Not yet. I'll try not to leave it too long though."

She nods tightly, her jaw hard as she fists her hands in the front of her baggy T-shirt. "Okay."

"Come here." I stick my arm out for her and pull her into my side.

Cody moved out a couple of weeks ago, and now I feel as though I'm committing the ultimate betrayal by leaving Mum on her own. She's a fighter though, and I know she'll be resilient through the transition to having the house to herself. Still, it sucks.

"I'll give you a call during the week, make sure you remembered to put the rubbish out on the right day," I tease.

She tickles me in the ribs, a sad yet content laugh falling from her lips. "Go on, you. Hit the road before you're stuck halfway through the pass when dinnertime calls."

"Yes, ma'am." I let her go, crossing the room to collect my duffle from where it sits packed against the skirting board. "Has Cody organised the guy to come get those donor cars out of the back yard?"

"Yeah. He said the man will turn up Thursday. I think he only gets one hundred dollars per car, but it'll be nice to have the full use of my section again."

"I bet."

"I thought about putting in a vegetable garden, but who am I going to feed when both my boys are gone?"

"Do one of those community patch things," I suggest.

She lifts her brows and tips her head in acknowledgement. The project would be right up her alley—giving back to those in need. We hit hard times after Dad left, and if anything, it gave Mum a new respect for the ways in which people pull together when you're on the bones of your arse like that. She tries where she can to repay the help she received, to assist women who are in the same situation as she was.

"Take care, Mum. Love you."

She crosses the kitchen to place a kiss to my cheek. "And you, Son."

She busies herself tidying some invisible speck on the counter top. I know she's doing it to avoid watching me leave, distract herself, but she'll be okay. I came back to tie things up, to set things straight, and these past few weeks I've done just that.

That's why it's time to move on. My work here is done. I literally did everything I came back for.

Except get a job.

A chill taints the air as I step out of the house and head to the car to throw my bag in the back. The indicators on the HQ flash—yeah, I bought it off Cody— as I unlock it. I've made a few upgrades to it, mostly the central locking I installed, and a new, better stereo system, but overall, it's still the same grey beast I broke down outside Cam's with.

Seemed only fitting it'd be the car I returned in, then.

Eight sessions with the shrink was all it took for her to uncouple me from my fear of failing and to push me gently in the direction I belong in. Every excuse I put up, she countered with a reasonable alternative.

My mum needs me: she was fine on her own before she had kids.

I'm supposed to find a job: they employ people in Burbank.

I have scheduled appointments with her: she could transfer my counselling to another shrink at another practice.

Cam and I are too different from each other: variety is the spice of life.

Apparently, hating the way somebody stores their belongings isn't a valid excuse not to be with them. Who would have thought? But then again, I did always know. Just like I know I did the right thing by leaving how I did. Giving Cam the space to breathe. Giving her a sign that no matter how long it takes for her to be ready to move on, I would be waiting.

If she's even found it.

I start the car with a healthy rumble, and idle out of Mum's driveway as I begin the trek back to the place I should have returned to weeks ago. I set myself a limit, made sure Cam would be the one to let me know she was completely ready to leave her past behind, but who was I kidding? How long did I really think I could wait?

Hopefully, it's not too late. Hopefully, she feels I'm worth a second chance.

Hopefully, she's still there.

THIRTY-ONE

CAMMIE

"I DON'T WANT IT, MUM." I THRUST THE PIECE OF notepaper back at her, frustrated that she just won't listen.

"Would you stop being so stubborn?" She pauses, glancing at the removal men who carry my solid oak sideboard toward the truck, and lowers her voice. "I've had enough of seeing you mope around the place when all it would take is one damn phone call to sort this out."

She snatches my wrist, wrestling me as I try to break free of her hold. I grit my teeth, forcing my hand into a fist so she can't try to give me the number again.

"You're behaving like a child," she says vehemently.

"Because you're treating me like one," I whisper-yell in return, eyeballing the men as they jostle the furniture around behind her.

My mother stares at me, her lips pursed. It's a look I haven't seen since I accidently spilled nail polish on her carpet as a kid.

Before I can predict her next move, she reaches out and shoves the paper down the cleavage of my top, into my bra.

"Mum!"

"Take it," she grits out, spinning away.

I retrieve Duke's number, ridiculously enraged that a slip of paper connected to him in some vague way has touched such an intimate part of me. I clear my throat, garnering Mum's attention as she heads for the house.

She turns, her head shaking slowly, her jaw hard as I lift the paper between us and shred it.

"Fine," she snaps, getting the attention of the removalists. "Wallow in your damn misery then." She tosses her hands in the air, marching back into the near-vacant house.

I'm pissed at her, partly because she won't let the issue go, but mostly because I'm redirecting the anger I feel at myself for not having the guts to do exactly what she says.

I should call him. Make a friendly gesture, and touch base to see how his job-hunt is going, how his family is. Yet the thorns in my heart twist in the septic wounds left by his touch, his kisses, when I think of how to *end* the call.

I'd be a love-struck teenager telling him, "No, you hang up first." I wouldn't be able to do it, especially if our conversation cemented the fact that there's no chance of there ever being an "us".

"We've only got the beds to go and then we're done," the older of the two removalists says, coming to stand beside me. He points to the way they've stacked the rest. "We can fit some of your boxes in the gaps if you know which ones you don't need right away."

The truck will sit loaded in their yard for two days

until I take ownership of my new property. Turns out Amanda knew her shit, and the house sold for a tidy profit within three weeks. Seeing Jared turn up on my doorstep with the contract and a celebratory bottle of wine cut the last tether I had to sanity, leaving me afloat in a sea of doubts.

The largest, that any life I create from here on in will ever be as good as what I once had.

Nine years ago, when I held Taylah in my arms for the first time, this isn't what I saw in my future. Standing alone on the porch of the house I thought I would die in didn't even cross my mind. I honestly fell in love with this place, believing I'd never leave. That I would spend the rest of my life making memories here with my daughter, my family, even grandchildren.

And yet, here I am, watching my possessions get bundled into the back of a truck, wondering how I'm going to fit them all into the new place. It's got the same number of rooms, but a smaller footprint. It's all I could afford, applying for a mortgage on my own.

"I'll go shift some boxes to the door here for you," I let the removalist know. "Make a pile that you can take from."

"That would be brilliant." He gives me a tight nod before relaying the message to his off-sider.

I head into Taylah's room to gather the couple that hold the belongings of hers I decided to keep. My eye catches the school uniform still hanging in the wardrobe. I need to donate it, but in the never-ending list of things to do when shifting house, I forgot.

"Cam?" Mum calls from the depths of the house.

"Yeah?" I drone back, still not over her performance

with the phone number.

"Do you have any blankets left out? I've pumped the airbed for you, so I thought I may as well put the bedding on it."

"Beside the French doors," I shout as I reach out and pull the uniform from the rail.

My hand hangs in mid air as I frown at how unusually heavy the blouse and skirt are. I step backward, intending to lay the outfit on the nearby boxes, when the reason for the added weight tumbles to the floor. *What on earth?*

"Where are you, Cam?" Mum calls from the hall.

"I'm in here." I squat and retrieve the notebook, turning it over as she appears at the door.

"Did you mean these ones?" Her eyes narrow as she spies what I have in my hand. "What's that?"

"I don't know. I just found it." I've got no idea what's inside, but I know one thing for sure: this notebook isn't mine. I've never had a grey one with the imprint of waves on the cover.

"Open it up." She gestures to the book with the blankets in her hands. "Whose is it?"

"I don't know." I murmur as I flip the front cover open. The handwriting is messy, masculine, but I know that it's not Jared's.

"I'll be in the kitchen when you're ready," Mum says softly. "I'll put the jug on—have a coffee ready to go."

"Thanks." I have a gut feeling that I might need a wine, though. My fingers track over the decorative text scribbled on the first page.

echoes in the storm

The handwriting is choppy, dark lines scratched over each other, evoking a sense of thunder and lightning, wind and hail. *Chaos.*

With the book held in my hands, I slowly fold my legs and drop to the floor in the strip of afternoon sun that spills in the window. The light illuminates the thin pages, showing the mass of writing behind. I turn the sheet over, my throat thick with apprehension as I prepare to dive in.

They say man's greatest enemy is himself, and I never understood the depth of that idea until I killed my first stranger in the name of freedom. You're repeatedly warned that you can never truly be prepared for how it feels to take another man's life. Of course, you bullshit yourself with the theory that you're out there to kill the bad guys, that you won't feel cruel because you're ridding the world of the evil scum that slights the face of the earth.

But then you shoot him. He doesn't die with the first bullet, of course, because you're new to this and, well, killing a man isn't quite the same as taking down a buck on your uncle's back block.

He barters, pleads with you, but you don't understand it all because the guy talks a whole different language. But you get the gist of it. You realise that you do care because this guy ... he's you. He's a man who fights for his ideals as well. A guy who fights for his country. His freedom.

And so the next guy you shoot, you spend a bit more time lining up, because fuck knows you don't want to hear that all over again. You get quicker, sharper, but not because you want to be the lean, mean, killing machine you fantasised over when you first enlisted. You do it because you don't want to fuck up. You don't want to hear their words, their cries.

Their humanity.

You disassociate to survive. Close off the parts of you that mean you feel compassion, love, and empathy. Lo and behold, you become a fucking universal soldier: robotic, detached, and clinical.

Yet, when you come home, that mindset doesn't magically vanish the second your foot hits home turf. It is you. You are the war, and you are death. Family, they see the change, and they try to connect. But nothing works, because of course you've shut down all channels to the things that used to make you happy, the things they know you like.

They don't know this new guy. Nobody does, least of all you.

He's a stranger to everyone.

That's where you came in, Cam.

I rest the book in my lap, my heart thundering in my ears. Closing my eyes, I will my pulse to ease off and concentrate on taking deep, equalising breaths.

It does stuff-all to help.

My finger twirls in the end of my hair as I continue with the journal Duke left for me, clearly knowing that one day, I would find it.

You were the echo in my storm. At first, all the little things you did differently irked at me. They niggled, annoying the shit out of me constantly. I thought it meant we couldn't get along, that there was no chance we'd work out. But you know what I figured out when Archie phoned to tell me the car was ready?

They were like the faint call of home, lost in the wind and the roar of thunder. It was you calling me, hoping I'd hear you and find my way out of the dark that I had lost myself in when I detached from life, when I shut off to survive.

You, Cam, were my echo. My call back.

And fuck it all if I didn't find home in the end.

A single drop hits the page, blurring the words I've yet to read. I dab at it with my sleeve before wiping my cheeks, panicked that I'll ruin even one of his precious words and miss what it is he wrote to me.

As I write this, I can hear you crying in your room. You think I left, but the truth is I made it as far as the end of the driveway. I stopped to check the road and found myself staring at the spot you told me Taylah lost her life.

I realised then that I couldn't leave you without telling you how you saved mine. But letting you know now, while you're upset and angry … you wouldn't believe me. You're mad I'm going home, and I get that, babe, I really do. But I think you need this as much as I do.

We both have loose ends to tie up before we'll get a proper chance at making it.

You need to stand on your own two feet for a while to remember how strong you are against the winds of change.

So this is me, in the dark with only my goddamn torch to light the page, thinking of where I can leave this so that you'll see the truth when you're ready to.

I know where. And if you've found it, it means you do now, too.

It means you are ready.

I'll be waiting for you, Cam. Waiting for you to

hear my echo.

"Mum!" The notebook hits the floor as I launch from the room, swinging myself through the doorways to find her where she said she'd be—in the kitchen. "Mum."

"What?" She sets her coffee mug down. "What's going on, Cam?"

"I need Duke's number," I pant.

Her face falls. My heart is crushed. "Oh, love. I deleted it after I wrote it down. I figured if you wouldn't take it today, you wouldn't ever need it."

I frown, looking around for her bag. "He phoned you, though. It'll be in your call history still as an unsaved number. Where's your bag?"

"In the car." She launches to her feet, hurrying out the door.

I jog after her, my heart beating so fast it's almost a solid vibration. The removalist spots me as I drop off the porch, bypassing the stairs, and heads over.

"We're done for the day, so unless you've got anything urgent, we'll be back in the morning to load up the last of it."

I glance over at the younger guy as he straps the bedframes to the side of the truck. "Uh, no. Thank you."

He offers a goodnight and heads to the rear of the truck as his offsider jumps to the ground.

I couldn't care less what they want to do. All I need is my mother's phone. She skids to a stop beside me, her Chucks kicking up dust in the gravel.

"Here. You do it. I don't know what to look for, or where to find that kind of information."

Despite my panic, I manage to chuckle as she passes her phone over. The removal truck pulls away while I unlock the screen. My finger swipes up, left, taps the screen again and again, but it's still not fast enough. I need it now. I need to call him and tell him that I hear his voice very fucking day, and I've only just figured out which way to go.

"Cam?" Mum asks, still beside me.

"Hang on."

"No, Cam." She nudges my arm.

I look into her eyes as the thunder of the storm grows louder, enough to drown out my erratic heartbeat banging a bass drum in my ears. Only it's not thunder—it's the rumble of a car that I never thought I'd hear again.

It's the sound of home coming to *me*.

THIRTY-TWO

DUKE

Fuck. She's sold the house. The anxiety I'd managed to get a lid on these past six weeks hammers to life in my chest as I turn up the driveway, only to be greeted with the grill of a huge fucking truck. *Jesus.*

I slam the HQ into reverse and backtrack to the road to let the guys out.

Just in time, I hope.

The second the truck clears the gateposts, I curve over the grass to get in behind the vehicle and pull up Cam's drive. My fingers beat to an imaginary rhythm on the steering wheel as I take the final bend around the trees and see the house come into view.

With her standing outside.

Thank fuck. Small miracles do happen.

Screw parking the car properly. Screw even turning the damn thing off. I shove the door open at the same time as I wrench the handbrake on, and step out to face the music.

Clara gives me a quick wave as she steps backward, and turns for her car. Her daughter, on the other hand ... I widen my stance to brace for Cam as she literally leaps the final half a metre between us.

"I heard you," she cries, burying her face in my neck as she wraps her arms and legs around me. "I heard your echo every day, Duke."

"You found it." Fuck that makes me happy. So fucking happy.

Cam pulls back, her hands on my face as I hold her to me. "Why are you here?" Her eyes search mine as her mum's car pulls away behind us.

"I couldn't wait any longer. It's been almost two months."

"I know." Her forehead touches mine as she closes her eyes. "I couldn't call." She pauses, swallowing hard. "I wanted to, but hell ..." Cam leans her head back, unshed tears caught in her lashes as she looks to the sky. "I couldn't bear to hear your voice again if you would have said that you didn't want me."

"Fuck, Cam." I drop her to the ground so she can stand. "I *do* want you. But you had to be sure. *I* had to be sure."

She simply smiles, her hand tracing the side of my neck as she watches it with a dreamy look in her eye. If I can give her reason to look that way day in, day out, then my future is in her hands. Where she goes, I'll follow.

"I missed you so much," she whispers. "It was hard at the start."

"Babe." I kiss the woman to bring her back to the present, soft and slow. "Don't take yourself back there. Let's just look forward, okay?"

"No." She frowns. "We need to get it all out there so we both understand."

This is where we differ. As much as I recognise that the past has shaped who I am now, I've realised that the future is entirely dependent on my attitude, whereas Cam places so much stock in what's gone by, as though the failures of her past dictate the choices of her future. It doesn't have to be like that.

"I didn't handle things well, Duke." She clings to the front of my shirt, her brow set in a hard line. "I got drunk; I did stupid shit." She laughs, bitter and short. "A few nights after you left, Susie and Bevan took me to the pub to try and loosen me up. They left me there with the little brother of a girl I went to school with."

"Cam ..." If this is going where I think it is ...

"I have to tell you, Duke." She closes her eyes and shakes her head. "Hear me out, please."

This woman realises I know how to kill without remorse, right?

"He brought me home."

I pry her hands off me, taking a step back. "Don't."

"Helped me get to bed."

"Stop it, Cam!" I pace back to the HQ; the engine is still running. *I could go. Just get in and go before she says it.*

"Listen to me, Duke!" she counters. "He put me to bed, offered to stay, and you know what I said?"

I don't want to hear it. I can't. "If you've got any ounce of respect left for me," I warn her, "you won't tell me."

"I said he should go because I'm in love with someone else."

What?

"Did you hear me, Duke?" she says, her footsteps

approaching. "I said I love you. I've known since then that there's no getting over you, just learning how to live without you."

She gasps as I spin and grab a hold of her sweater to pull her to me. "Tell me again. Tell me to my face."

Cam twitches a smile, inching closer. "I love you, Duke."

"Fuck, Cam. I'd be stupid not to tell you that I love you, too." Her eyes fill with unshed tears as I take her face in my hands. "I knew that the second I walked back up your driveway in the dark, no light, to write you that damn note."

"No torch at all?" she asks.

"No torch." I trace her cheekbones with my thumbs, memorising everything about her in this moment. "I was so focused on you, on saying the right thing, that I didn't care. Didn't think twice about it."

She laces her hands behind my head and pulls me to her, but it doesn't take much; I was thinking the same thing. Her kiss has more vigour this time, more urgency, as she runs her tongue across mine. Her taste, her smell, her touch—they all overload my senses as I bring the moment I've thought about to life in vivid colour.

We've made it through the storm. We've followed the echoes and found each other in the midst of all that chaos.

She's my oasis amongst the rage and anger. My safe place.

"Tell me," I say, pulling away. "Where are you going?"

"Huh?" Her hands slip to my chest.

"The house—you sold it."

"*We* sold it." I see the regret in her gaze, and yet what makes me proud is the determination that also shines through in her words. "I bought a place a half hour from here. Smaller, but everything I need." She smiles, her gaze lifting to meet mine again. "And you know what? I'm actually looking forward to doing the whole redecorating thing again."

"Let me guess," I tease. "White and grey?"

She rolls her eyes with a smile. "What else?"

I go to kiss her again, yet she pushes out of my arms, her eyes wide.

"You have to come see this. The moving guys left it until tomorrow, saying they didn't want the heavy furniture to break it." She beckons toward the house. "Come."

Of course I go. I'd follow this woman into war unarmed.

Cam darts up the steps and into the house, dashing left into the living room. She points to the same wall the door is on, meaning I have to swing around to see what she gestures to.

For the first time in my life, I almost cry.

Framed in ornate white wood is a large print photograph. The picture itself is monochrome, yet it's the depth of the black that strikes me. A white sailboat adrift on a stormy black sea.

"Do you like it?" Cam asks quietly.

I can see that she looks at me in my periphery, yet I can't tear my eyes from the silver nameplate mounted on the mat board that edges the picture.

"The Duke and Duchess"

In the boat are two tiny figures, clinging to each other in the middle of the vessel, a royal insignia on the sail.

"Where did you find it?" I move closer, fearful that if I look away now I'm going to miss another important detail.

"I went down a bit of a rabbit hole while I was looking up design ideas for the new place, and somehow I ended up on this website for a guy who sells bespoke pieces." She snorts a little laugh. "It cost almost as much to freight it as it did to buy it."

"It's priceless." *Because it's us.*

She edges closer to slip her hand in mine. "You asked me if I believed in fate, Duke. I think this answers that—don't you?" Cam lifts her free hand to gesture to the image.

Fuck, it's more than fate. It was a series of events that individually held no meaning, but that together, meant everything. It was the game board of our lives laid out for us to take. We were two pieces chasing each other along the path, yet never resting in the same square until six weeks ago when I broke down. All we had to do was the roll the dice enough times to make it to the end to be together.

"Where are we going to hang it?"

"We?" Her brow twitches as she looks up at me.

All or nothing; dive into the black, Duke. "Everything important that I own is in that car, Cam. I came here with the intention to stay." My heart kicks up pace. "Hopefully with you."

"You came back to live with me?" The panic is clear in her eyes, the worry that she's misunderstood what

I've said.

"If you'll have me."

"Duke ..." She tips her head to the side, giving me a "what do you think?" stare.

"So what now?" I slip my hands onto her waist, loving how she feels back in my hold. How the hell did I have the strength to walk away from this? How crazy *was* I?

"Now," Cam says, pushing to her toes to place a kiss to my lips. "We go to bed and spend one last night here for old times' sake."

"Old times," I chuckle. "It was only a couple of months ago, Cam."

She smirks, tugging on my hand to lead me to her room. "It may as well have been a lifetime without you, Duke."

THIRTY-THREE

CAMMIE

I BOUGHT THAT IMAGE THINKING IT SIGNIFIED the two of us trying to hold on despite the fact that the odds were against us and there was no way we could have ever made it. I thought it perfectly catalogued how we were doomed from the start. Who would have thought I would show it to the man I love and have him ask where *we* would hang it?

"Cam." Duke tugs on my hand as I turn left into the hallway.

"What? Don't tell me you've had an epiphany and you're changing your mind about this, buddy, because I told you I loved you, and whether you realise it or not, that means you're mine, for good."

He gives me that sexy little I'm-not-really-smiling grin that I've missed. "As much as I love to hear you talk a hundred miles an hour again, just shut up for a second, would you?"

I lift an eyebrow, dropping his hand to cross my arms.

"I just wanted to say"—he backs toward the door—"that I need to turn the car off."

"Oh, crap. Of course."

Duke reaches out to snag my hand again, tugging me flush against him. "So," he damn near growls. "Get this sexy little butt into bed and be ready for me, because I swear to God, I'll have that car off and locked in record time."

"Get to it, soldier." I back out of his hold and give him a playful push on the chest.

He laughs, turning heel and jogging out the door to sort the car. My pulse races as I turn in the opposite direction and hustle to my room, my sweater off by the time I'm through the door. The HQ still runs as I strip my off leggings and tank. Only when I unclip my bra does the engine finally shut off. *Record time, my arse.*

I lie back on the airbed to wait for him, switching positions half a dozen times to try and find the most flattering and alluring one. The minutes pass, and I finally give in to check my phone. *What the hell?* How long does it take to walk back inside, shut the door, and then come screw me senseless?

As much as I try not to worry, the devil on my shoulder gets the best of me, and I find myself tugging my clothes back on. Voices drift up the hallway once I round the bedroom door, both of them deep and definitely male.

I reach the front door and sigh at the sight of his black truck in the driveway. "What are you doing here, Jared?"

Both men turn to look at me with a frown. *Weird.* I feel as though I'm an intruder on my own property.

"It's all right, Cam. Go back inside," *Jared* assures me. *Weirder still.*

"You two talking out here like old friends doesn't make any sense, guys." I try a casual laugh, but it comes off as more of a nervous giggle.

"We're having a bit of a chat, Cam," Duke tells me. "Nothing to worry about. I'll be right in." His tone says otherwise.

I hesitate, hoping they'll ignore me and carry on with their conversation, yet the two of them stare me down until I take a few steps back toward the door. What whacked up alternate universe have I just stepped into if *these* two men are having a discussion that doesn't require me?

Horny and frustrated, I stomp back down to the bedroom and sit on the end of my lonely airbed, cross-legged. My phone spends more time lit up than it does asleep, given I constantly check the time.

Five minutes pass, then ten, but it's close to fifteen before I hear the snick of the front door followed by the click of the deadbolt and the faint rumble of Jared's truck.

Duke rounds the doorway, his head down, a hell of a lot less fired up and ready to ravage me than he was before my ex turned up.

"What did he want?" I ask, straightening my legs out.

"Came over to check how the move went, make sure you're set to be out on time." He sighs. "Dickhead doesn't trust you to do anything yourself, does he?"

"No, but that hardly constituted you two talking for twenty minutes," I bite back.

Duke's fingers dab his bottom lip as he drops a short, "Huh."

"It's a legitimate point," I protest. "The least you can

do is tell me the truth about what was said."

"The truth," Duke says, stalking into the room, "is we spent less than two minutes talking about you moving house. He then spent somewhere around five telling me why you're not worth my time, probably in an attempt to sabotage any chance at you being happy." He drops to his knees at the edge of the mattress. "Which leaves about thirteen minutes, if I'm counting right." I notice why he touched his lip; the skin is split, fresh blood dotted around it. "I guess I wasted about ten of those calmly and coolly reminding him that he's got no business being involved in your life anymore, because well, you know, you've sold the house, so that's the end of that." Duke lifts an eyebrow as I reach out and touch the flesh under his split lip. "Final three minutes, babe?"

"Yes?"

"I spent those reminding him all the things there are to love about you, that *I* appreciate, and that he'll miss out on because he wasn't man enough to be there for you when you needed him most."

"Duke," I whisper, touching his lip. "What did you do?"

"Got rid of the competition so I could mark *my* territory in peace." He knocks me on my back, promptly tugging my leggings off. "Told him I had better things to do than waste my time on him, and that he could stick around if he wanted, but that I wasn't into that kind of kink."

"You did not," I counter.

"How do you think I got the split lip?" Duke wrestles my sweater off next to find I never put my bra back on. "Fuck, Cam."

"Well," I say, lifting my eyebrows as I stretch out beneath him, "according to you this is all yours, so have at it, soldier."

"Fucking 'ey, it's mine." He ducks down to suck one of my nipples into his mouth.

I moan at the exquisite feel of his hot lips on me, and at the word replaying through my mind: *mine.* There's something carnal about the way Duke says it. As much as I'm an independent woman, it makes me want to submit to this man in every way—I love that.

"Don't leave me again," I say, threading my fingers into his hair. "I couldn't survive if you did."

He crawls over me until we're face to face. "I'm not going anywhere, babe. Not unless you're coming with me."

And I believe him, because after all, he came back. It broke my heart at the time. Hell, it still tears me apart when I think about how I felt hearing him leave that night. But I can see his reasons clearly now. The storm has passed, the clouds have lifted, and the sun is shining brilliantly what we have. I never would have been able to see how bright our future is with the clouds of regret forever over our heads. We each needed to settle our pasts, accept our losses, and come into this with a clear head to give it a fair chance.

I run my hand through Duke's hair as he lays hot kisses between my thighs, thankful that we're here, however hard the road was.

A few short months ago, I sat in my living room wondering if there ever was such a thing as love. Wondering if I would ever really know how that felt again, or if I was doomed to vanquish the emotion to the furthest reaches of my memories.

Today, I can say without a doubt that I believe in love again.

EPILOGUE

DUKE

"What the fuck have I done, Cody?" My hands ache with my frustration. I clench them into fists to save from tearing the fabric in my hands to shreds.

"I can't believe you were in the army, bro, and you still can't get a Windsor knot right."

"There were ways around it." I jut my chin out of the way as my little brother wrestles my tie into submission. "How much time do we have?"

"Plenty." He tugs the tie tight, and then pats me on the shoulder. "Stop stressing. You've literally got to walk out the door and you're there."

Still. Doesn't keep me from panicking that I'm going to fuck this up.

Cam didn't want a church wedding.

She gave me one of her signature lectures about how she's not religious, and so having one wouldn't make sense, somehow, putting in one hundred words what she could have said in twenty.

I christened the kitchen counter with her the second she shut her goddamn mouth.

Turns out the things that used to drive me crazy about her drive me crazy *for* her now.

"Ready?" Cody slaps me on the shoulder.

"I think so."

He laughs at the clear panic on my face. "Bro, you do realise you've been married before, right? This isn't your first rodeo."

"No, it's not. But it's my first with Cam, and I want it to be perfect for her." I check my reflection, making sure the collar of my shirt sits perfectly beneath the lapels of my dress uniform jacket.

I can't deny the pride that chokes me every time I lay eyes on the medals displayed on my chest. I only wish there could have been more, because that would have meant I was able to *do* more.

"Come on then." Cody stands off to the side with his hands slung casually in his dress pants. The smile on his face chokes me up worse than I already am.

He's proud. Fuck, he wasn't proud when I went to war, let alone when I came home alive.

"You've done good, Brother," he says with the barest twitch of a smile. "You've done good."

I give him a slap on the shoulder and a tight nod as I pass by and head out to kick the day off.

True to form, Cam and I planned this wedding in mere months. Our whole relationship has been a whirlwind of sorts, but I think my mum summed it up best when she said, "You've simply got lost time to make up for."

Who would have thought that when I returned to New Zealand a mere fraction of the man I was when I left, that somewhere out there in this great country, a woman was enduring a personal hell of her own, a woman that would one day be mine?

I shake my head in disbelief as I make the short walk out of the old stone house and down the manicured lawn to the spot where our family and friends wait. Hushes sweep the guests when they spot Cody and me making our way to our spots at the "altar".

Cam's father gives me a slow nod as I pass by, that simple gesture meaning so much more than he'd ever know. I went old school, asking him for his daughter's hand, and he gave his blessing, telling me that I should have come into her life a few years earlier.

Fuck, if I could have, I would have, without a doubt.

A murmur sweeps the crowd, people turning their heads to look at where Cam will make her entrance. My gut twists into a tight fist, my heart picking up its pace.

"She's here," Cody helpfully whispers in my ear.

"I know, jackass," I hiss back at him, assuming the position. "She's early."

My baby couldn't wait, either.

Music begins to play, but all I can hear is the repeated *whomp-whomp* of my heartbeat as I wait on my future wife.

I haven't seen her for two days while she stayed at her Mum's to go through the final preparations. It's the longest we've been apart since I returned to her house with a boot-load of possessions and a heart full of hope.

Two days too long. Two days I'll never get back.

But as she rounds the hedge to walk through the archway, it's two days' worth the sacrifice.

She's fucking perfect in every way.

And so fucking mine.

Mrs Duke Harwood.
Cammie Harwood.
Fuck that sounds good.

ALSO BY MAX

FALLEN ACES MC SERIES

Unrequited
Unbreakable
Tormented
Existential
Misguided

COMING SOON
Redundant

BUTCHER BOYS SERIES

Devil You Know
Devil on Your Back
Devil May Care
Devil in the Detail
Devil Smoke

BANJAXED SERIES

Pistol
Loaded
Recoil

STANDALONE

Malaise
Tough Love

THE MUSIC

Listen to the songs that inspired the book on my playlist, Echoes in the Storm, on Spotify.

"Anesthesia" – Type O Negative
"Imagine" – A Perfect Circle
"Hang on to This" – Days of the New
"Words as Weapons" - Seether
"Let it Die" – Foo Fighters
"Soldier of Fortune" – Deep Purple
"Hero of War" – Rise Against
"Dirty Road" – Days of the New
"Drift" – Emily Osment
"I Don't Wanna Be Me" – Type O Negative
"Trenches" – Pop Evil
"Nearly Forgot My Broken Heart" – Chris Cornell
"Shade" – Silverchair
"Letters Home from the Garden of Stone" – Everlast
"Heavy" – Collective Soul
"Wicked Game" – Stone Sour
"Wars" - Hurt

ABOUT MAX

Born and bred in Canterbury, New Zealand, Max now resides with her family in beautiful and sunny Queensland, Australia.

Life with two young children can be hectic at times, and although she may not write as often as she would like, Max wouldn't change a thing.

In her down time, Max can be found at her local gym, brain-storming through a session with the weights. If not, she's probably out drooling over one of many classic cars on show that she wishes she owned.

FOR ALL UPDATES AND ANNOUNCEMENTS –
SIGN UP TO MAX'S NEWSLETTER:
http://bit.ly/2mr9BUs

FOLLOW MAX

FACEBOOK – PROFILE
www.facebook.com/max.henry.9003

FACEBOOK – PAGE
www.facebook.com/MaxHenryAuthor

GOODREADS
www.goodreads.com/author/show/
7555353.Max_Henry

TWITTER & INSTAGRAM:
@maxhenryauthor

FOR EXCLUSIVE NEWS AND EXCERPTS -
JOIN MAX'S FAN GROUP, THE MADHOUSE!
www.facebook.com/groups/346994535466425/